ANIMAL INVESTIGATORS:
MISSION 2

GHOST DOGS

His whole body tensed. In the long grass he saw eyes. Eyes gleaming red in the dark. He saw more of them. There! And there! And shapes, slinking through the shadows. Lean, sinewy shapes with smooth lizard heads and long gazelle legs, twisting like wraiths in and out of the trees.

"It's them," breathed Ellis. "The ghost dogs."

He felt an icy chill down his spine. He thought it was his fear. But then he realized, I'm so cold. The air temperature was plummeting. His fingertips were tingling. His face stung. That shouldn't be happening on such a warm, summer night...

SUSAN GATES worked as a teacher in Africa and then in England before becoming a full-time writer. She has since had over one hundred books published and, among other prizes, has won the Sheffield Book Award twice and been commended for the Carnegie Medal.

Susan is married with a daughter and two sons, and lives in County Durham.

ANIMAL INVESTIGATORS:
MISSION 2

GHOST DOGS

SUSAN GATES

USBORNE

To Laura, Alex and Chris

First published in the UK in 2008 by Usborne Publishing Ltd.,
Usborne House, 83-85 Saffron Hill, London EC1N 8RT, England.
www.usborne.com

Copyright © Susan Gates, 2008

A CIP catalogue record for this book is available from the British Library.

JFMAMJJAS ND/07   ISBN 9780746085769   Printed in Great Britain.

CHαPTⒺR One

The boy came skidding into the kitchen of the children's care home. The cook looked up from the soup he was stirring.

"Hey," the cook greeted the boy. "What's your hurry? She after you again?"

She was the matron of the children's care home. She hated the boy. She saw it as her personal duty to civilize him.

Leon the cook was his only protector. Every time the boy was in trouble with the matron, he ran to Leon in the kitchen. Or, sometimes, he ran to the kennel outside and curled up with Tyson, the care home dog.

The boy was about four years old. No one knew his age exactly because he'd been dumped, two years ago, outside the care home. He'd had a piece of paper pinned to his coat. It said, *Look after him. His name is Blue.*

That had annoyed the matron right away. "Why is he called Blue?" she'd said. "What kind of stupid name is that for a boy?"

Blue sat down at the kitchen table.

"Want a drink?" asked Leon.

Blue nodded. He could speak, as well as any other four year old. But he didn't often choose to.

Leon poured Blue some milk into a plastic mug. The old man liked Blue. But even he had to admit that the boy was strange. Even stranger than the matron realized. She hated Blue because of his defiance – the way he stared at her with those icy blue eyes, as if she was something nasty he'd trodden in. But, if she'd known about what else he did, she'd have had a fit.

"Don't try any of your tricks now," Leon warned Blue. "*She* might come in. Remember, they're a secret between you and me."

Blue stared back at him. His eyes made even Leon shiver. They chilled you right through to the bone. Apart from that, he looked like a nice, normal little boy. His nails were kept clean, his hair short, his face well-scrubbed, like all the other care home kids.

But he wasn't normal. Normal kids couldn't do what Blue was doing now.

"Hey, I told you not to do that stuff," said Leon. But it was no good. Blue never took any notice. He just stared at you and did what he liked. That's what made Matron so mad, made her want to break his spirit.

Blue had turned his gaze to his milk. He stuck a spoon in it. Then fixed the mug with those frosty eyes. And the milk froze. It turned solid. Blue knocked it out of the mug onto the table. And using the spoon as a stick, he licked it, like a lollipop.

"How d'you do that?" the cook marvelled. Frost shimmered on the table too, as if Blue had made his own mini winter.

Blue shrugged. He had no idea where his strange powers came from.

"Heck of a party trick," said the cook, shaking his head and grinning.

The kitchen door flew open. "What's going on here?" Matron's suspicious gaze swept round the kitchen. She saw Blue eating his lollipop. "Why aren't you at school?" she demanded.

Blue shot her a scornful look, then wriggled out of the open kitchen window.

"That boy!" said the matron. "He'll be the death of me."

She caught up with Blue out in the yard. He'd gone to his second refuge, the dog kennel. He was curled up inside, with Tyson, the old Alsatian.

"Come out of there!" ordered Matron, kneeling down.

She reached into the kennel and hauled Tyson out, by his collar. It was a worn red collar, with a metal tag on it, engraved with his name and the care home address.

"You old bag of bones," she said to Tyson. "It's about time we had you put down. You're half dead anyway."

Then Matron made an even bigger mistake. In her bad temper, she slapped the old dog on the nose. Tyson yelped, piteously.

Blue came crawling out of the kennel. He stood up.

"Now I've got you," said the matron. "And don't stare at me like that! Like you want to kill me!"

But Blue never took his eyes off her. Suddenly, Matron felt the air around her getting chilly. Which was strange because it was a blazing hot summer's day. She felt something cold on her lips, in her hair. White flakes whirled around her. Surely it couldn't be? Not snowflakes? Then she was shivering, her teeth chattering. Her breath turned to crackling ice crystals. She watched in horror, as her own hands turned blue.

A last crazy thought flashed through her head. *So that's why they named him Blue.*

Then her eyes glazed over and she slumped to the ground.

Blue took one quick look at the matron's body, dusted with snow. Then he said, "Come on, Tyson. Let's go."

The boy and the dog took off down the road.

They crossed a bridge over a river. Then passed a sign that said, *Welcome to Forest Edge. Please Drive Carefully.*

Blue didn't want to go to the town. He wanted to get as far away from people as possible. But, first, he took off his shirt and sweater, his socks, shoes and jeans, and put them in a neat pile on the riverbank.

Then he and Tyson turned right, went down a dirt track and plunged into the forest. Soon, the trees swallowed them up.

CHAPTER TWO
FIVE YEARS LATER

Ellis Straker was bored. He was in the garden, behind the city's Natural History Museum, where he lived with his guardian, Professor Talltrees. Ever since the start of the school holidays things had been quiet. There'd been no missions to go on, no animal mysteries to solve. In any case, Meriel wasn't around. Professor Talltrees was her guardian, too. Together, she and Ellis made a formidable team.

Ellis was an ace tracker and Meriel had even more amazing powers – she could read animals' minds. But Meriel had done one of her disappearing acts.

Ellis sighed. *When's she coming back?* he wondered.

Meriel could be a real headache. Even the Prof called her unpredictable. Some people had called her a freak – more animal than human. But Ellis missed her a lot. Things always got lively when Meriel was around.

She'll turn up when she wants to, thought Ellis.

Ellis worried when Meriel went walkabout. But there was no stopping her when she got restless and needed space to roam wild and free.

Suddenly, Ellis forgot about being bored. He kneeled down on the grass. All his senses were instantly alert. He'd seen something – Ellis, with his sharp tracker's eyes, saw the tiniest animal signs that others missed.

He picked up an owl pellet. Every so often owls sicked them up, with the indigestible bits of their last meal inside. Ellis crumbled the pellet in his hand. Bones, fur, tiny sharp teeth scattered across his palm. He brushed them off.

He glanced at the tree branch above his head. It was white with owl droppings. It looked as if an owl perched there often.

What does it come here for? wondered Ellis. What did it hunt every night? Mice maybe?

He scanned the ground for clues.

"Hey," he murmured. He'd spotted something. There were greasy rings around a twig. Ellis scraped off some grease, rubbed it between his fingers. It was quite fresh, probably made last night. He smelled it and grinned.

It's not mice. It's rats! thought Ellis. They'd twisted their long, slippery tails around the twig.

He was on the rats' trail now. On hands and knees he searched the ground, like a detective looking for clues. He found chewed twigs, the rub marks their bodies made on stones. Here were their prints – like tiny four-fingered hands, with claws. They led to a flat stone.

Got you, thought Ellis. He'd found the nest. He put his ear to the stone – he could hear a faint scrabbling underneath.

Carefully, he lifted up the stone. There was a dark tunnel entrance. It seemed far too tiny for a rat to enter – but Ellis knew that a rat could collapse its skeleton and squeeze through a wedding ring. Their teeth could gnaw through concrete and steel. He took out the tiny pencil torch he always carried, shone it down the hole.

"Hi there," he said.

Surprised rat eyes glowed back at him. He moved his torch around. In the beam, he saw a nest made of chewed-up plastic bags with pink wriggling rat babies in it. The rats started squeaking. Ellis snapped off his torch.

Rats were a huge problem in the city. They were everywhere, living off the garbage humans left. If the council knew about these, they'd be poisoned straight away. But Ellis wasn't going to tell.

"Have a nice day," he told the rats. "But watch out for that owl tonight." Then, gently, he put the stone back.

As he stood up, he heard loud voices. They were coming up through a grill from the basement. That was where the Prof had his laboratory, where he studied the bones of extinct animals. The voices seemed to be arguing. Ellis recognized one – it was his guardian's. But he'd never heard the other.

Ellis's immediate thought was, *Is the Prof in danger?*

Like Meriel, Ellis had massive respect for his guardian. Although, to others, the Prof seemed a grave and forbidding boffin, Ellis had grown to love him, like a father.

Ellis went into the building at a run.

He clattered down stone steps and raced along the long corridor that led to the Prof's lab. The corridor was lined with cloudy old specimen jars. A pickled octopus stared from one. In the next were the coiled guts of a pig. Ellis sprinted past. He could hear the voices clearly now, coming through the open lab door.

One, the Prof's, stayed calm and cool. "I told you, I never go out on missions. Not since my accident."

The other voice insisted, "But that's not good enough! It's you I want and you've got to come quick! Or we'll be too late!" It sounded to Ellis like a teenage boy. A teenager full of attitude and aggression. Who wouldn't take no for an answer.

Ellis burst into the lab. "Anything wrong, Professor?" he asked. "I heard shouting."

Professor Talltrees limped from behind his lab bench. He was tall, lanky and grey-haired. Along with his lame leg, he had other old wounds. Scars puckered the left side of his face. He wore a black eyepatch, to hide the empty socket where, years ago, he'd had his injured left eye removed.

The Prof told Ellis, "It's all right, there's no problem." He introduced his visitor. "This is JJ – Jay Harding Junior. His dad, Jay Harding Senior, is an old friend of mine. You've heard of his dad, I suppose?"

"Yeah," shrugged Ellis. Everyone had heard of Jay Harding Senior.

Jay Harding Senior's son looked about sixteen. And Ellis already didn't like him, for showing the Prof disrespect.

Just who does he think he is? thought Ellis.

Ellis didn't bother looking at JJ's face. Instead he checked out his shoes. He always did that when he met people, in case he had to track them down later. JJ's shoes were customized trainers, with his name in silver down the sides. They must have cost a bomb, like his designer jeans. *Flash, loud-mouthed, arrogant rich kid*, thought Ellis.

He was guessing about the rest, but there was no

doubt Jay was rich. JJ's dad was a billionaire press baron. He owned lots of newspapers, all over the country. He had the reputation of being a very tough man to deal with.

JJ ignored Ellis completely. He was still trying to make the Prof change his mind. "I need a top animal expert. And that's you. Right? I've heard Dad talk about you – he says you're the best. If money's the problem, I've got plenty. I'll pay you."

JJ fished a fat wallet out of his jeans pocket. He pulled out a wad of notes, waved them around.

The Prof's voice changed. It was still polite. But now it had an edge of steel. "Put your money away," he said, carefully keeping his anger under control.

Under the Prof's severe gaze, JJ frowned. But, for once, he did what he was told.

"It's not about money," continued the Prof. "It's about the skills you need. And you said you need a tracker—"

"Yeah, I do!" interrupted JJ, who couldn't seem to keep quiet for two seconds. "I need him to go into the forest. There's this town called Forest Edge. But the people there are so dumb! They daren't go into the forest. They say it's haunted!"

"Haunted by what?" asked Ellis.

JJ swung round. His look dismissed Ellis as unimportant, but he answered him anyway. "By dogs," he answered. "Ghost dogs."

"The ghosts of greyhounds, Ellis," added the Prof. "Greyhounds that have been taken into the forest and killed by a local man."

"They call him Hunter," JJ butted in. "He's really mean."

Then JJ suddenly realized. He did a double take. "Wait a minute!" he bawled. "Is this the Ellis you were telling me about – the brilliant tracker? You never said he was a twelve-year-old kid!"

"Thirteen," corrected Ellis.

"And you want me to take him with me?" JJ was going to add more objections. But there was something about Ellis's steady grey eyes, his watchful stare, that stopped him.

"I strongly advise it," the Prof was saying, "if you want to get the evidence you need to convict this man Hunter of poisoning greyhounds."

"Poisoning?" said Ellis. He didn't like to hear of animals being poisoned. Not even rats.

"Yeah! The Prof here says it could be by deadly

nightshade. He's just shown me a picture of it," said JJ, waving his hand at a book lying open on the lab bench.

"Look, hadn't you better tell Ellis the whole story?" interrupted the Prof. "Then he can decide whether he wants to take on this mission."

"Decide?" said JJ, who seemed amazed that Ellis had any say in the matter. "Tell him he's got to. You're his dad, aren't you?"

But the Prof shook his head. "No, he hasn't got to. It's his choice. And besides, I'm not his father."

JJ looked fit to burst with frustration. But he turned to Ellis. "Okay, it's like this. My dad's making me work for the summer on this small-town newspaper, *The Forest Edge Echo*. Dad said I've got to learn about his business the hard way. He said, 'There's no favouritism just because you're my son.' Anyway, I sniffed out this big story…"

Ellis was listening hard. Despite himself, he was interested.

But then JJ threw his arms in the air, waved them around. "Look, I haven't got time for this! We've got to get to the forest before tonight. We've got to get that evidence. And stop more dogs from dying! You coming or not?"

Ellis hesitated. He didn't want to spend more time than he had to with this obnoxious kid. But at the same time, he could feel rage beginning to burn inside him, at what was happening to those greyhounds.

"Okay," Ellis told JJ, "I'll go."

"Can you track in the dark?" asked JJ. "And without anyone seeing you?"

Ellis looked at him scornfully. "Is that a serious question?"

Ellis had grown up in Africa, where he'd lived with his parents on a wildlife reserve. He'd learned his skills from Gift, the best African tracker around. Together they'd tracked animals and people in all sorts of conditions – in the dark, in desert sand, even over bare rocks.

"Only asking," said JJ. "Anyhow, I'll explain my plan on the way. We're taking my plane, of course."

"Your plane?" said Ellis, trying not to look impressed.

"Well, it's Dad's actually. Just his little four-seater, not his private jet," said JJ. "It's out at the airport. It'll take us right to the forest."

"I'll go and pack some stuff," said Ellis. "It'll only take ten minutes."

"I'll be waiting outside in the taxi," said JJ.

"You've got a taxi outside, with the meter running?" said Ellis. "It'll cost you a small fortune!"

But Ellis already knew what JJ was going to reply. "That's not a problem," said the rich kid, shrugging. "My dad's got loads to spare."

Chapter Three

Ellis peered out of the plane window. Clouds drifted past, centimetres from the tip of his nose. Sometimes they parted and he glimpsed a bright yellow wing and wing struts. But that's about all there was to see.

They'd left the city far behind and were flying north, to the little town of Forest Edge and its haunted forest. Estimated time of arrival – 6 p.m.

The plane dropped like a stone, then steadied. Ellis's stomach lurched. He'd been in big planes before, but this was a much bumpier ride. And scarier, too. The plane seemed so dinky, almost like a toy, or something a girl would put on a charm bracelet. It seemed far too tiny and frail to be up here, all on its own, in this big wide sky.

JJ was strapped into the front seat, next to the pilot. "Can't this thing fly any faster?" he said. The pilot pulled out the throttle, banked left. The engine growled, like a noisy car.

The pilot had been silent so far. But now he spoke for the first time. "There's bad weather ahead. You sure your father authorized this flight?"

JJ's voice got shriller, like an angry toddler's. "You questioning me? You'd better quit that *now*, or else I'll tell my dad. Your job is to get us to that forest before dark. That's all you need to worry about."

JJ sounded like a spoiled, bullying brat.

Alone in the back seat, Ellis was turning over in his mind the things JJ had told him as the taxi sped to the airport. JJ had explained a bit more about the mission. About how he was working as a junior reporter on *The Forest Edge Echo* when he got an anonymous letter. It told him about a man called Hunter. Hunter lived in a shack just outside the forest. He killed greyhounds for a living. He took them into the forest and poisoned them. They were racing greyhounds who didn't win races any more, and their owners wanted to get rid of them. So they paid Hunter to do it. The whole town knew it was going on. It had been going on for years. But no one dared stop it because Hunter was dangerous, a really scary guy. Everyone in Forest Edge kept well out of his way and let him get on with his business.

"But I'm going to nail him!" JJ had told Ellis, excitedly. "He's going to be on the front page of the paper. I can see the headline now: *DOG POISONER BROUGHT TO JUSTICE BY JAY HARDING JUNIOR.*"

And JJ had also told Ellis something else. "It'll make a great story!" he'd said. "Dad'll be proud of me, for once. It'll prove to him that I can make a success of something."

"Have you told your dad about it?" Ellis had asked.

"Uh, no," JJ had admitted. "I want to surprise

him. Anyway, it's really hard to see my dad. I have to make an appointment, through his secretary."

"You have to make *an appointment*? To see your own dad?" Ellis had said, shocked.

"Yeah, well, my dad's a very important guy," JJ had said defensively. "He's got a newspaper empire to run. I never know where he is. He might be in New York, Paris..."

The little plane rocked and shuddered as they hit some more air turbulence.

Urggh! thought Ellis, as he almost threw up his breakfast.

"Storm ahead," said the pilot.

Suddenly, the plane was tossed about, as if it was being shaken inside a giant paper bag.

"I'm climbing," said the pilot, his voice sounding urgent.

He yanked on the wheel. The engine noise rose to a shriek. Ellis felt his backbone slam into his seat as the plane tipped onto its tail, seemed to claw its way upward.

The tiny plane levelled out again in calmer air.

Phew, thought Ellis. He'd always hated being trapped in cramped spaces. It was his worst nightmare. He screwed his eyes tight shut, waited for the queasy feeling to pass.

Ignoring the pilot's warning – "Hey, that's not safe!" – JJ undid his seat belt. He scrambled into the empty back seat, beside Ellis. He had a can of Coke in his hand. "Want some?" he asked Ellis.

Ellis shook his head.

"You okay?" asked JJ. "You've gone white as a sheet."

"Course I'm okay," said Ellis. The wave of sickness had passed. And JJ was asking him something.

"Anyway, what's your dad do?"

"My dad's dead," said Ellis. His gruff tone warned JJ, *Back off. Don't ask me any more questions.* And, this time, even JJ kept quiet.

But in Ellis's mind, it seemed like a dam had burst. Memories came flooding back, of the day two years ago, when his parents had been killed by poachers on the wildlife reserve. Gift had found them. He'd told Ellis, "Don't go into the house." Ellis had gone into the bush on his own to grieve. When he'd staggered out, days later, the Prof and Meriel had been waiting for him.

Ellis swallowed hard, to get rid of the lump in his throat. It took all his willpower to focus again on the mission.

He asked JJ, "So what's my part in nailing this dog-killing guy? What's your plan?"

"It's simple," said JJ. "Tonight Hunter takes another greyhound into the forest."

"How do you know?" asked Ellis.

"Because I've been keeping him under surveillance. This morning, just after dawn, he brought a dog back to his shack. It's always the same. He brings them back in the morning. And that same night, he takes them into the forest to poison them."

"So I track him into the forest?" said Ellis. "Tonight, when he takes the dog? And try to stop him?"

"No way!" said JJ. "He's a violent guy. He carries knives. You track him, but you don't let him see you."

"So what *do* I do?" asked Ellis.

"You find the dog's body," said JJ. "While Hunter's gone, I'm going to search his shack. Bet I find poison there. And when the poison matches up with the stuff in the dog's body, we've got our evidence. It'll be the biggest story *The Forest Edge Echo* has ever run! With pictures!" said JJ, excitedly. "Look at this one I got this morning."

And he pulled a digital camera out of his pocket. On the tiny screen were even tinier figures – a beautiful brindled greyhound trotting beside a huge guy in camouflage gear. Ellis couldn't see any more details – the photo was taken from a distance. But he could tell that the dog wasn't cringing or scared. It obviously had no idea what lay in store.

"I heard him shout her name – she's called Star," said JJ.

"She's still a young dog," said Ellis, shocked. He'd somehow thought the dogs Hunter poisoned would be old and sick. "There's nothing wrong with her."

"She might be just three or four years old," said JJ. "I looked it up on the net. That's when greyhounds mostly stop winning."

Ellis felt another surge of fury inside him. *What a waste*, he was thinking. Star could live another ten years, maybe longer. He checked out Hunter's feet in the photo. It was hard to tell – but he seemed to be wearing big combat boots.

You'll be easy to track, Ellis thought, with a grim smile of satisfaction.

"Hope my photo's good enough to put in the paper," JJ was fretting, as he put his camera away. "I was a long way away, hidden in some bushes."

Ellis thought, *Does he care about Star at all*? All he seemed to care about was getting a big scoop, so his dad would be proud of him.

"So what do you think of my plan? Brilliant or what?" JJ bragged.

Ellis could see a hundred holes in JJ's plan. For instance, what was he supposed to do when he found Star's body? Drag it all the way back? If he left it in the forest overnight he'd have to bury it deep, or wild animals would find it. But none of those details really mattered because he'd already decided – he wasn't going to let Star die, just so JJ could get some evidence.

No way, Ellis thought privately. *That's not going to happen*. He didn't know yet how he was going to save Star. He just knew he had to.

While he was thinking about this, JJ was jabbering, "People in town really believe in those ghost dogs. They say that at night all the dogs

Hunter's poisoned roam around the forest." JJ laughed scornfully. "Can you believe that?"

He threw his head back, took another swig of drink. "You don't believe in ghosts, do you?" he asked Ellis.

Ellis barely had time to say, "No," before the pilot shouted back. "Stash away any loose gear!"

Ellis rammed his backpack into the locker under his seat. He looked out the window. The bad weather had caught up with them. Storm clouds raced towards them at dizzying speed. It went dark as they swallowed the little plane. A fierce blast of rain slammed into the window, as if trying to smash it in. Thunder crashed, the plane rocked wildly. A jagged lightning bolt split the clouds and lit the heavens for a second. The plane seemed to be adrift in a boiling black sea.

"Hang on!" yelled the pilot.

And then it was chaos. With lightning sizzling around it, the little plane was punched by a mighty fist. It staggered in the sky, then suddenly fell, in a stomach-churning drop. JJ's drink can was torn out of his hand. It clattered off the walls and drink sprayed over the pilot.

"I said no loose gear!" screamed the pilot.

The can came flying back. Ellis's arm shot out and caught it, just before it bounced off his face.

The pilot cursed as he fought to keep control. Ellis was flung against his straps, as the little plane bucked like a rodeo pony. The wind seemed to be trying to rip it apart.

Again they plunged. Beside him JJ was shouting and screaming, as if he could order the storm to let them go. But Ellis thought, *This is it*. He imagined them spiralling helplessly down, smashing into the ground, wreckage scattering for a kilometre around.

Then, as suddenly as it had started, it stopped.

The plane gave a final shudder. The last tatters of black cloud whisked away. Then they flew out of the storm into sunshine.

For a long time, no one spoke. Even JJ was silent. Ellis found he'd scrunched the drink can into a twisted mess. He said, "Nice flying," to the pilot.

The pilot nodded, then crouched back over the controls.

JJ said, "That's Forest Edge."

Ellis looked down. Far below, he saw a little town,

on the edge of a vast, hilly forest. Several rivers and streams ran through the hills, like silver ribbons. And there was a lake at the forest's centre, winking up like a big, shiny eye.

Then, as Ellis watched, the light faded and a gloomy shadow was pulled over the forest like a shroud.

Ellis thought, *Looks like the kind of place that could be haunted.* Until he remembered that he didn't believe in ghosts.

"The sun's setting!" fumed JJ. "We're late!" His plan was already beginning to fall apart.

"Listen," said the pilot, "with that storm, it's a miracle we're here at all."

JJ gave the pilot his orders. "See that shack? That's where we want to be. But land well away from it, like behind those trees, so Hunter won't see or hear us."

In the twilight, the pilot put the plane down in a grassy clearing. It jolted along to a stop. JJ jumped out, mad with impatience.

"Hunter's probably gone into the forest by now. Can you still track him?"

Ellis said, "Sure."

Once, he and Gift had tracked a poacher who'd killed a leopard. Even though his boot prints were three days old. They'd found the leopard's skin hidden in his backpack.

But Ellis blocked out those memories immediately. He didn't want to start thinking about Africa again.

JJ said, "Come on! Let's get going."

But Ellis was already running. A picture flashed through his mind – of a trusting, doe-eyed greyhound that had no idea it was being led to its death. Because of the storm, too much time had been lost. It could be too late to save Star...

He heard JJ yelling something behind him, but he didn't stop. He was sick of listening to what JJ wanted. He was going to do this his own way.

He could see Hunter's shack now. He suddenly ducked behind a pile of logs. What if JJ was wrong and Hunter hadn't gone yet?

But the shack looked dark, deserted. And Ellis didn't have time to be as cautious as he should. He sprang up and went closer, searching for fresh footprints. He found them straight away – the deep imprint of Hunter's big boots, with a dog's paw prints, fainter, beside them. They were heading for the forest and they'd only just been made.

There's still a chance, thought Ellis. A chance he could get to Star in time.

Suddenly he stopped dead, his whole body quivering. He'd nearly missed it, the nylon rope in the grass. He kneeled down. The rope was well hidden. Very carefully, Ellis brushed the dirt off the top and revealed a noose.

"A spring trap," breathed Ellis.

He hadn't seen one for years. But this one wasn't meant to catch animals – it was meant to catch people. Ellis knew what to look for now. His eyes followed the rope to a stake, driven into the ground. Then to a birch tree, bent almost double. If he stepped in the noose, the stake would jerk out, the birch spring up, the noose tighten round his leg. And he'd be whipped high into the air and left dangling helplessly.

JJ came creeping up. He glanced fearfully at the shack. "Has he gone?"

"Yes," said Ellis. "But keep back. He's booby-trapped the place."

"That's what I was trying to tell you," said JJ.

"Everyone in Forest Edge knows about it. It stops people prowling around his property. That's why I daren't get too close this morning."

In the fading light, Ellis looked around. "There's one over there," he said, pointing to a circle of lighter coloured grass. "It's a pit trap. And there's probably others around." He didn't have time to check. Every minute counted, if he was going to save Star's life.

"Keep your phone switched on," Ellis told JJ, as he hurried towards the forest. "I'll keep in touch."

JJ said, "You can't. There's no mobile coverage out here. We'll meet up later, right?" He gazed around for a landmark. "See that big boulder over there? The one that's leaning sideways? I'll wait for you there, after I've searched the shack."

Ellis said, "Okay". But was he even listening? He glanced at the rock. But then his eyes locked again on those prints.

"Want to take my camera?" asked JJ. "It's got night vision – you might get some good pictures. But make sure Hunter doesn't see you."

This time Ellis did look up.

"Pictures of what?" said Ellis.

"Uh, of Hunter, you know, actually giving the dog poison. That'd be the best evidence ever!"

"Yeah, I know," Ellis burst out, "it'd look great in the paper. Bet your dad would be proud. You're sick, JJ!"

Ellis plunged into the forest, while JJ was left holding his camera, staring after him.

CHAPTER FOUR

Ellis knew this wasn't a good way to track. Tracking needs a clear head. But he couldn't control his emotions. He was full of frantic worry for Star. And furious, too – with Hunter, with Star's owners for wanting her dead because she'd stopped winning races, with JJ for only caring about his newspaper scoop.

He tried to calm himself down and concentrate.

In his present mood he might miss the trail, make mistakes.

It was getting harder now. The dirt track had ended and Hunter and Star were walking on grass. But at least it was a clear night. Moonlight splashed the forest floor and made it easy to see. A mosquito whined in the warm summer night.

Gotcha, thought Ellis, slapping his neck.

Suddenly, he dropped to all fours, scurried between the trees like a squirrel.

He'd seen where Hunter's big boots had crushed the pine needles. Hunter was striding confidently, like he owned the forest. Like he didn't need to be sneaky because he knew no one would dare interfere with his business.

Where had they gone now? There! Ellis climbed a hillside, searching desperately. He saw a snapped twig. They'd turned right, down a narrow, ferny path that led along a ridge.

Where was Hunter taking Star? How deep in the forest would he go before he fed her poison? He hadn't done it yet. On a patch of sandy soil Ellis picked out Star's footprints. Star was trotting along, like a happy dog. She thought she was out for a walk.

Ellis saw Star in his mind – her neat pointy head, her long legs, like a gazelle. You couldn't see it in JJ's photo, but Ellis just knew her eyes would be gentle and trusting. He shook his head to get rid of that image. He couldn't afford to let it cloud his mind.

His nostrils wrinkled. Tobacco smoke! Instinctively he dived into the ferns. Someone was coming. Ellis cursed himself for being careless. He'd almost let himself get caught.

He peered through the ferns. His worst fears were realized – it was Hunter, swaggering along the path, whistling between puffs on his cigarette. And he was on his own.

A whole riot of thoughts ripped through Ellis's mind. *He's done it. He's poisoned Star!* Rage boiled inside him. He almost flung himself at Hunter, screaming, "You murderer!" He only just managed to control himself. Shaking, he stayed crouched in his hiding place.

Then he thought of JJ, searching the shack. Had he finished yet? If he hadn't, Hunter might walk in on him.

I could run back, thought Ellis, *and warn him*.

Hunter was walking with a slow, steady tread. Ellis could easily beat him back.

But what about Star? Ellis's common sense told him, *She's dead already.* But what if she wasn't? Common sense said, *Even if she isn't, she will be soon. And what can you do to save her?* But on this mission, Ellis wasn't listening to his sensible side. He decided that JJ would have to look after himself.

He watched Hunter stride down the slope and disappear. He waited until the smell of his cigarette had gone. Then Ellis sprang up and set off again, back-tracking Hunter's footprints, deeper and deeper into the forest.

Inside Hunter's shack, JJ shivered. *I can't wait to get out of this creepy place.*

Hunter's trophies were everywhere. A stuffed deer head hung on the wall. Its glassy eyes glistened in the moonlight flooding through the windows. On a table was a badger skull made into a lamp. And animal skins from all the creatures Hunter had trapped were flung over the chairs.

It had been easy to get in. The front door wasn't

even locked. Hunter probably thought, *Who'd dare to rob me?*

JJ opened a drawer. *"Yuk!"* There were more grisly trophies inside – a withered snake's head and a fox's tail.

JJ slid the drawer shut. He knew he should get out soon, in case Hunter came back. But he didn't want to go without some evidence. He was desperate to prove himself, to make a big success of this newspaper job. If he did, he thought his father might notice him. Might make a space for him in his busy, important life. Might, maybe, even love him.

JJ looked around the shadowy shack. Where hadn't he searched? Prof. Talltrees had said Hunter might use a natural poison, like deadly nightshade, so it would be hard to prove the dog hadn't eaten it by accident. He'd told JJ all Hunter would have to do was crush up the berries in doggy treats.

JJ went into the kitchen. And there it was, in a pot on the window sill – a sinister-looking plant with shiny black berries, just like the picture the Prof had shown him.

"Deadly nightshade," murmured JJ. "You were

right, Professor." And he gave the Prof a silent salute.

JJ took a photo of the plant on Hunter's window sill. Then he took a sample, wrapped it up in a twist of tinfoil, stashed it away in his pocket.

He was washing his hands carefully in the kitchen sink, when he happened to glance out of the window.

"Oh no," he breathed.

His heart had been fluttering before. But now it went manic, like wild, beating wings.

Hunter was striding towards the shack's back door. JJ whirled round, hurtled back across the living room and shot out through the front door.

His mind was shrieking at him, *Run! Run!*

Like a hunted animal, he tore across the moonlit scrubland. He was racing for the cover of the trees. Then he saw the tilting boulder, where he'd said he'd meet Ellis. So he swerved and sprinted for that instead.

Halfway there, he dived, panting, behind a gorse bush. He peeped out. Hunter was nowhere in sight.

Then JJ spotted him. He gave a great, shuddering sigh of relief. The dog killer wasn't chasing him. He hadn't even gone into his shack. He was heading away from it, towards Forest Edge, probably to the pub. He wouldn't be back for hours.

He never even saw me! thought JJ, triumphantly. *What an idiot!*

His panic forgotten, JJ strolled towards the boulder. He stepped beneath it. It loomed above him, made a nice little shelter. *I'll wait here for Ellis,* he thought.

He felt really pleased with himself. After a shaky start, his plan had gone brilliantly. He'd got his part of the evidence – the photo and the poison sample. It was all down to Ellis now, to track down the dog's body. That was crucial. Without it, they wouldn't have a case.

JJ thought, *He'd better be as good as the Prof says.*

There was a log in front of him, standing upright, like a pillar.

JJ wondered, briefly, who'd put it there. But who cared? It made a convenient backrest. JJ slouched against it. Immediately, it shifted.

Whaaaa...? thought JJ, springing away. The boulder above him juddered.

JJ's gaze shot upwards. At the top, the log had been sharpened, like a giant pencil. And on that slender point the whole weight of the boulder rested, balanced skilfully, so the slightest touch would bring it down.

The boulder shifted again with a terrible grinding noise. It began to topple. The log stopped it, but it was cracking under the strain.

It's a trap! thought JJ, still staring upwards, frozen with horror.

At the last second his survival instinct took over. He tried to dive out of the way. But the log supporting the rock splintered, then snapped in two and the boulder came crashing down.

In the forest, Ellis had found the place where Hunter had poisoned Star. He could tell by the tracks. Hunter's boots had scuffled around. Then he'd turned and left, on his own. But where was Star? She'd probably staggered off, curled up somewhere. Ellis tried to search for her tracks. But he couldn't see straight because his eyes were bleary with tears.

Stop it! Ellis warned himself. He rubbed his eyes savagely, bit his lip, to stop it trembling. He felt he'd failed Star. He knew he probably wouldn't find her alive. He was even scared to, because what could he do? He'd just have to watch her suffer. But he ordered himself, *Don't you dare give up!* His mission now was to find her body. It was crucial evidence to help convict Hunter.

So, with grim determination, he forced himself onwards, looking for signs of the dying dog. He was marking his way now, with lolly sticks he had in his backpack. Usually he could remember his route home, map it out in his head. But in a pine forest like this all the paths looked the same. He drove another lolly stick into the ground.

Still kneeling, he got out his torch, flicked the beam around.

There! he thought. It was a hair on a twig. It looked like it could be one of Star's. Then Ellis found a scoop under the bush, where she'd rested, the slide in the grass where she'd crawled.

He heard water burbling nearby – one of the streams he'd seen from the plane. There was a lake somewhere, too, he remembered.

Maybe Star's headed for water, he thought. *The poison might make her thirsty*.

Then he noticed something else. His face creased up with surprise and confusion.

What's that? he wondered.

He crouched down to look. He'd found a small pyramid of round pebbles. They were river pebbles, washed smooth by water. Poking out of the top was a forked stick. And hanging from the stick was a collar, its red colour faded. Was this the grave of someone's pet dog? What was it doing here, way out in the forest?

Propped against the pyramid were flowers – tall, purple foxgloves.

Ellis smelled them, felt the petals. They were quite fresh, maybe put there this morning.

Ellis frowned, puzzled. He stared round uneasily. The grave looked like it had been here for years. But who'd left the fresh flowers? Could it be Hunter?

Naa, thought Ellis. No way could he see Hunter doing that.

And, according to JJ, people from the town were too scared to come into the forest.

The whole thing spooked him. But he was in a

hurry. He was going to grab the dog's collar, take it with him. But something stopped him. If it *was* a grave, it seemed disrespectful. So, by the light of his torch beam, Ellis just read the metal tag. He had to scrape off green moss to do it.

Tyson, said the tag, *Forest Edge Children's Care Home.*

Then, from somewhere quite close by, Ellis heard a howl – a long eerie call that made his flesh creep.

Star? he thought. He sprang up, scattering foxgloves.

He raced through a tangle of light and shadows. Then suddenly he was out on a shore. His gaze swept round a lake, silver with moon glow. On the opposite shore a waterfall tumbled down cliffs and hit the lake with a roaring sound, sending up clouds of spray. To his left, water flowed from the lake into a stream, the one he'd heard burbling just now through the trees.

Ellis put his torch away. He didn't need it now. The moonlight and sparkling lake made it almost as bright as day.

Then he saw the dog, lying on smooth, rounded pebbles, near the water's edge. It was Star – you couldn't mistake her, with that brindled coat. She wasn't moving at all. Her eyes were shut.

She's dead, thought Ellis. It was how he'd expected to find her. But it was still a shock.

Ellis ran down to her. He reached out a trembling hand to touch her. She felt freezing! As cold as a slab of ice. Ellis drew back his hand in surprise – he hadn't expected that. Her body should still be warm. Ellis shook his head, baffled. But there was one thing for sure. It wasn't Star who'd howled just now.

Then Ellis's head shot up. There was that howl again. It made the hairs at the back of his neck prickle.

Where's it coming from? he thought.

He saw grasses ripple further along the shore. Instinctively he backed away from Star and crouched behind a dead, washed-up tree. There was a quivering, deep in his stomach.

Maybe the Forest Edge people were right about this place. Maybe it *was* haunted by ghost dogs.

Come on! Ellis told himself. *It's just scary stories*.

Another howl came, a different one. Then another. From over there! Ellis's head whipped round.

Whatever was howling was surrounding him, moving in. He crouched lower, peering through the white, dead twigs.

His sharp tracker's ears heard rustling in the grasses, a twig snapping. He realized he was shaking.

Get a grip, Ellis! he told himself savagely.

He peered out from his hiding place. The shore where Star lay was dappled with shadows. He shifted his gaze across the lake to the waterfall. Was that a cave behind the tumbling water? He couldn't be sure.

But then his whole body tensed. In the long grass he saw eyes. Eyes gleaming red in the dark. He saw more of them. There! And there! And shapes, slinking through the shadows. Lean, sinewy shapes with smooth lizard heads and long gazelle legs, twisting like wraiths in and out of the trees.

"It's them," breathed Ellis. "The ghost dogs."

Maybe they'd come for Star, to join their ghostly pack.

He felt an icy chill down his spine. He thought it was his fear. But then he realized, *I'm so cold*.

The air temperature was plummeting. His fingertips were tingling. His face stung. That shouldn't be happening on such a warm, summer night.

Now a white, thin mist was creeping across the lake. It drifted over Star's body. The pebbles on the shore were suddenly shiny, like jewels. Ellis stared at them in total confusion. That couldn't be ice glazing them, could it? Then the mist reached him where he crouched, hiding. Ellis tasted it on his tongue. It had ice crystals in it. The air temperature had to be well below zero. Right before his eyes, he saw his own warm breath turn into white clouds.

Then he saw, where the water met the bank, a thin sheet of ice begin to form, pushing out in ferny shapes into the water, like frost patterns on a windowpane.

What happened next he saw only through freezing white haze. A creature came crawling out of the mist. Ellis strained his eyes to see. It was on all fours like a dog. But it wasn't a dog. It didn't look human, either. Long tangled hair covered its face. Rabbit skins were tied round its body.

Ellis rubbed his eyes, as if they were playing tricks. He put a hand to his head. Was this some kind of nightmare? The mist made it all the more eerie and dreamlike.

The creature scuttled up to Star. Ellis's eyes were locked on it now, trying to see as the mist swirled and parted. He didn't notice that, on the dead tree he hid behind, tiny icicles were forming.

The creature crouched over Star's corpse. Her body was rigid; there were ice crystals in her fur. Ellis watched, horrified: *What's it doing to her?*

The creature got a stick from somewhere. It forced Star's jaws apart and stuck the stick down her throat.

Ellis tried to shout, "No!" But the word stayed frozen inside him. What was that ghoul doing now?

The stick must be hollow, because the creature was stuffing something inside. For a few seconds, mist hid the scene. When it parted, the creature was blowing down the tube, as if it was forcing something down into Star's stomach.

The reaction was almost immediate. Through the misty veil, Ellis saw Star's body jerk.

She's alive! thought Ellis, amazed and bewildered.

Star's legs twitched and thrashed the air. Then

she started dragging herself over the pebbles. She crawled down to the water's edge. Ellis could hear her, retching into the water, the creature squatting, froglike, beside her. It didn't hurt her. It was stroking her, holding her head, as if to comfort her.

Ellis stood up. "Hey!" he yelled. "Hey!" He couldn't form the words properly. His lips felt stiff, almost paralysed.

For the first time, the creature turned its shaggy head towards him.

It's a boy, thought Ellis. Through its matted hair, Ellis saw two pale, frosty eyes. They seemed to cut through him like laser beams.

Suddenly Ellis realized he wasn't just cold, he was freezing. His fingers were turning blue.

Through the mist came a soft growling sound. Something was springing over the pebbles. The wild boy was coming to get him.

Ellis tried to get away. At first his legs wouldn't support him. Then, with a stumbling, lurching run, he escaped into the trees. He ran and ran until he couldn't run any more.

He stopped, doubled up in a clearing, gasping for breath. Gradually the pounding in his ears faded, the red mist before his eyes began to clear. He stared at his hands. They were pink again. The air around him was warm. Fireflies danced, like little golden sparks around his head.

Something crunched under his foot. He looked down. It was a lolly stick. By sheer luck, he'd found the trail he'd left. He tried to calm his whirling brain, concentrate on tracking. The little white sticks guided him back to where Hunter had poisoned Star. After that it was easy. He just followed the prints of Hunter's great big combat boots.

At last, he stumbled out of the forest. He'd hit the meeting place almost exactly. *There's JJ!* thought Ellis.

He seemed to be resting, near the boulder.

Ellis ran towards him, words spilling out of his mouth. "Guess what? I just saw this real, live feral boy in the forest. Like, on all fours, like an animal, wearing rabbit skins!"

Then he realized two things at once. The tilted boulder had fallen. And JJ wasn't resting. His face was screwed up with pain.

"What happened?" asked Ellis, kneeling down beside him.

But he didn't need to be told, he could see at a glance. The fallen boulder, the snapped log, told him that Hunter had set a deadfall trap, a trap where a rock is rigged to come crashing down at the slightest disturbance. And JJ had walked right into it.

"Where were you?" moaned JJ. "Run to Forest Edge. Tell them to get here quick! Tell them Jay Harding's son is dying!"

Chapter Five

Ellis woke up late the next day. He was back home, in the Natural History Museum, in his own bedroom.

As he surfaced from sleep, for a minute his mind was blank. Then the events of last night came rushing back – Hunter, Star, the feral boy. It was hard to believe all that had really happened.

It had turned out that JJ wasn't dying. He'd just

broken his ankle. He was in hospital now in Forest Edge.

Ellis had wanted to stick around. He'd wanted to go back into the forest to look for Star, to see that wild child again and those other dogs. Ellis wasn't a mystical person like Meriel. He liked things to be logical, clear. As a tracker, he trusted only what his eyes told him. The trouble was, he still didn't know what exactly he'd seen.

But JJ hadn't given Ellis the chance to make any further investigations. From his hospital bed, he'd called the pilot of his father's plane to pick Ellis up, fly him back to the city.

Ellis had tried to see JJ, to argue, "My job's not finished." But the nurses had said, "I'm afraid he won't see you." It was as if Ellis had suddenly become a nuisance, as if JJ wanted him out of the way.

Dawn was breaking as Ellis flew back into the city. The sky was a blaze of fiery red. He'd taken the metro back home from the airport. He'd been almost asleep on his feet. The Prof was already in his lab; he never seemed to sleep much. Ellis had told his guardian some of what had happened. But he was swaying with weariness. "Get some rest," the Prof had told him. "You can tell me later." So Ellis had stumbled to his bedroom and fallen asleep without even taking his clothes off, sprawled on top of his duvet.

Ellis groaned and lifted himself up on one elbow. He should be trying to make sense of last night – what he'd seen in the forest. But his brain just didn't want to deal with it. It was all too weird, too scary.

Ellis focused one bleary eye. The Prof had a flat in the great rambling museum building, and Ellis's room looked out onto the garden. What he saw out there made him wake up instantly. There was a girl among the trees. She was small, skinny, dark-haired. She looked younger than her thirteen years.

"Meriel's back!" cried Ellis, leaping off the bed.

Meriel was usually darting about, quick as a dragonfly – she was a restless spirit. But now she was perfectly still, gazing at nothing, in a trance. Ellis grinned; he knew what that meant. Meriel was lost inside some animal's mind, seeing what it saw, feeling what it felt, thinking its thoughts. He wondered what creature it was. Not a squirrel – that would be far too boring. Maybe that owl was roosting in its favourite tree? Meriel liked animals that were fierce, that had some attitude. Preferably predators.

Then Ellis grinned again. He could see a flat stone at her feet, that she'd moved aside.

Along with predators, Meriel liked creatures that most humans hate. Creatures that aren't cute and cuddly. That have a really bad image problem.

Rats! decided Ellis. *That's what she's mind-reading.*

He hurried out into the garden to meet her.

Meriel was as still as a waxwork. But her mind was somewhere else, in the mother rat's body, bounding down the alley at the back of the museum in broad daylight, bold as anything.

Sniff, sniff. Meriel felt the mother rat's excitement. What was that smell? Food! Her whiskers quivered. She shoved her head inside a smelly garbage bag, dragged out a yogurt pot, stuck her head inside that, licked it all round. Then licked her paws.

Off again, scurrying close to walls. She knew this

alley, it was her regular rat run. *Sniff, sniff*. That was her own smell, from yesterday. She peed again, to make it stronger, then bounded off to gnaw at a chicken bone.

"Meriel!" said Ellis. "Stop messing about. I need to talk to you."

Meriel's body shivered. The light came back into her eyes. She stared at Ellis, with that familiar proud, defiant look.

"Rats are happy," she announced, as if daring him to disagree. "Rats have a really great time."

"Yeah, yeah," said Ellis. "Good for them."

"And they couldn't care less about people." Meriel threw back her head and laughed approvingly. "They're not even scared. Guess what? I just ran right over some woman's shoes. Should have heard her scream!"

"Meriel!" begged Ellis. "I've got some really important things to tell you!"

Meriel pushed the flat stone back over the nest with her foot. She fixed Ellis with her fierce, unblinking stare that, even after two years of knowing her, still unnerved him. As always, she got straight to the point.

"The Prof said you saw a wild boy in the forest. A boy who lives with dogs. I want to meet him. We've got to go today, *right now*. You slept for ages! I wanted to wake you up, but the Prof said wait..."

Ellis heard someone behind him – someone dragging their left leg.

"Hello, Prof," he said, without turning round.

Their guardian was taking a break from studying dinosaur bones. "Come into the kitchen," said the Prof. "And tell us both the whole story."

"Fascinating," said Prof. Talltrees, after Ellis had finished.

Ellis nodded. Like every good tracker, Ellis had an excellent memory. He'd told the Prof and Meriel every little detail – right down to the name and address on the dog collar and the foxglove flowers on the little pebble pyramid.

"Fascinating," said the Prof again. He leaned back in his chair. His gaze was faraway but with one hand he was gently stroking the scars on his face. Ellis and Meriel glanced at each other. They knew what that meant – it meant their guardian was deep in thought.

Meriel sprang up from her seat, paced about the kitchen like a caged tiger. On the cupboard was a little telly with its sound switched off. Meriel liked to watch the pictures flashing by – she thought mostly in pictures, like animals do. But today even that didn't calm her. Ellis had never seen her so tense and twitchy. This wild boy story really seemed to have got to her. Ellis was surprised by that. Meriel wasn't often interested in humans. Apart from the Prof and Ellis, only wild animals earned her respect.

Finally Ellis couldn't bear the wait either. He begged the Prof, "So what do you think?"

"Well, I don't think all those greyhounds were ghosts for a start," said the Prof.

"Neither did I!" said Ellis defensively. "Well, not *seriously*."

"I think what you saw was a true feral child, who's living in the forest with dogs. It wouldn't be the first case." And here, the Prof shot Meriel a look. Ellis noticed it, but he didn't know what it meant. There was a special bond between the Prof and Meriel that Ellis couldn't quite work out. He knew

Meriel had been with the Prof longer than him. But her past before that was a mystery. Ellis knew almost nothing about it – only that Meriel, like him, was an orphan.

The Prof continued, "I think what you saw was the boy saving Star's life. Shooting some kind of antidote down the tube into her stomach. Almost certainly made from forest herbs or plants—"

Ellis interrupted, "So, you mean Star's *definitely* alive?"

"I'd bet money on it," said the Prof. "And if he did that with her, it seems reasonable to conclude that he saved all the other greyhounds the same way, after Hunter left them in the forest to die."

Ellis shook his head in amazement. "That kid's a hero. I'd like to shake his hand!"

The shock of seeing the wild boy for the first time and those weird, icy eyes was fading now. Ellis was even thinking, *Why did you run? He was just some poor harmless feral kid.*

The Prof was still rubbing that scar. "I wonder what he used. Obviously something to make the dog vomit. And the foxgloves you saw – that's interesting. Foxgloves are really powerful plants. There's a medicine made from them that can actually restart your heart—"

Again Ellis butted in. He hated questions he couldn't answer, and, right now, his brain was bursting with them.

"But who *is* this wild kid? Where *does* he come from?"

"I can't answer that," said the Prof.

"So how come he knows all that stuff, about plant medicines?"

"Maybe he just learned from watching wild creatures," the Prof suggested. "If they're sick, they eat medicinal plants. That's well known."

"And what about that freaky cold weather?" Ellis reminded the Prof.

"That's weird," the Prof agreed. "But it probably helped save Star's life. It stopped the poison being absorbed into her system. That far below freezing, her body would shut down completely. Her heart would stop beating – so maybe this wild boy used foxgloves to restart it. Very clever!"

A shriek from Meriel made them both jump.

"Look!" she cried. She'd stopped pacing and was pointing to the television. A caption was rolling across the bottom of the screen. Ellis stared at it, stunned. It read, *Forest Edge Wild Boy. Local Reporter's Amazing Story.*

And there was JJ on the telly, smiling bravely, his ankle in plaster, leaning on a crutch. An interviewer was next to him, holding a mike.

Ellis dived at the set, turned up the volume.

"I didn't believe these stories that the forest was haunted," JJ was saying. "So I went in to see for myself. And that's when I saw the wild boy. He was on all fours like an animal, dressed in rabbit skins! I went after him, of course. But I broke my ankle and had to give up."

"You liar!" Ellis shouted furiously at the screen. He was furious with himself too. He thought, *I shouldn't have told JJ what I saw!*

It seemed JJ had forgotten all about Star being poisoned – a wild boy in the forest was a much bigger scoop. He never mentioned the other greyhounds either.

That's because I never told him about them, Ellis realized. *Or about what I saw the wild boy doing to Star.*

That gave him a little comfort. At least he hadn't

blurted out everything.

But the interviewer had turned to someone else now – a severe-looking woman in a grey trouser suit. He introduced her. "And here is Dr. Christine Summers, an expert in child psychology."

"Of course," commented Dr. Summers, "this poor, vulnerable child must be captured, for his own good. He must be trained to mix with other children and take his place in society. That's the best thing for him."

A great howl of rage came from Meriel, like a wolf defending its cubs. "The best thing for him!" shrieked Meriel, dancing with rage. "Stupid woman! How does she know what's best for him?

"Shut up! Shut up!" Meriel told the child expert, her eyes flashing fire. But when Dr. Christine Summers wouldn't stop talking, Meriel grabbed the remote and shut off the sound.

She spun round to Ellis and the Prof. "We've got to get to him!" she yelled. "We've got to get to him before they do!"

She went rushing out of the room. "I'm going NOW!" she yelled back at them. "Just as soon as I've got my stuff together!"

Ellis stared after her. He'd seen Meriel in tempers before, but never like this. It was a good job Dr. Summers wasn't here in the kitchen. Meriel would have clawed her eyes out.

Meriel whirled back into the room like a mini-cyclone. "And don't try to stop me," she yelled at them both, before she disappeared again.

The Prof was used to Meriel's sudden flare-ups. Usually he didn't even raise an eyebrow. But now, even he looked worried.

"Why is she so worked up about this?" Ellis asked the Prof.

The Prof hesitated. He looked uneasy, rubbing at the scars on his face. Then he finally said, "It brings back memories for her."

"What?" said Ellis. "You mean bad memories?"

"I'm not sure," the Prof admitted. "They might be good memories. In fact, that's what I'm scared of."

Ellis frowned. "What's that mean? I don't understand."

The Prof looked even more uneasy, as if he'd said too much.

"You can't not tell me now," Ellis protested. "Not if it's important for this mission."

Still the Prof hesitated. It seemed he was debating with himself.

Ellis said, impatiently, "Well, are you going to tell me or what?"

The Prof made a decision. "I suppose you had to know sooner or later," he sighed. "The thing is, when I found Meriel, she was two years old. And, well, er, the fact is, she was living with wild dogs. She was like that boy you saw – on all fours, growling, with long shaggy hair."

"You're kidding me!" said Ellis, amazed. "How'd that happen?"

"She was shipwrecked," said the Prof, "when she was just a baby. No one knows exactly what happened. But she was on a boat with her mum and dad, in the South Atlantic, off the Skeleton Coast of Namibia. And the boat sank. Meriel got washed ashore somehow. A wild dog pack took her in, fed her. They saved her life. And that's where I found her, over a year later."

Ellis said, "Wow! So what about her parents?"

"They didn't survive," said the Prof.

"Did you know them?" asked Ellis.

"I knew her mum. She was an expert diver, who

made films about sharks." The Prof took a deep breath. "Actually, the truth is, I was in love with her. But, in the end, she left me and married someone else."

"That's tough," murmured Ellis, half embarrassed, half fascinated by this glimpse into the Prof's private life.

"Anyway," said the Prof, ploughing on, as if he was determined to finish what he'd started. "Then she and the man she married had a child, Meriel. Meriel was born with the power to read animals' minds. She inherited it from her father."

"Her father?" echoed Ellis, amazed. He'd always wondered where Meriel got those mind-reading skills. He was itching to know more about Meriel's mysterious dad. Had the Prof known him too? But he didn't dare ask. It was clearly very painful for the Prof to talk about this part of his past. If Ellis pestered him with too many questions, he might clam up altogether.

So he just shut up and listened.

"Her mum's body was found quite quickly," said the Prof. He tried to carry on, but there was a strange choking catch in his voice. He had to swallow hard to get rid of it.

"Her dad was never found," the Prof continued, after a few seconds. "He was presumed drowned. Then I learned that I'd been named Meriel's guardian in her mum's will. So I went looking for her, and I kept on looking, long after everyone else had given up. I don't know why, I just knew she was still alive."

"How'd you find her?" Ellis said, forgetting he wasn't going to interrupt.

But the Prof didn't seem to mind. His voice was back to normal now. "I used to do a lot of canoeing then," he answered. "So I canoed all along that coast, into all the little bays and inlets, until I found her. I can still remember the shock – she was crouching on the rocks, blood running down her chin, tearing at a gazelle's thigh bone."

"How'd you know it was her?" asked Ellis, fascinated.

"Because, even under all the dirt and blood, she looked like her mum," said the Prof, shortly.

"Did she want to be rescued?"

"Hardly!" said the Prof. "Meriel barked, called the other dogs to help her. They were her family now. The mother dog attacked me, as if she was defending one of her pups."

"Did the mother dog blind you?" asked Ellis, glancing at the Prof's eyepatch.

The Prof hesitated again. He didn't like lying – but this was something he'd never told anyone. He said, finally, "No, Meriel did it. She fought like a demon. She clawed my eyeball. Later I had to have my eye removed, in hospital."

"That's terrible!" Ellis burst out furiously. "How could she?"

"You mustn't blame her," said the Prof angrily, his one good eye glaring at Ellis. "I don't want her blamed! She was a baby, she didn't know what she was doing!"

"Sorry," Ellis apologized, startled by the Prof's sudden, furious outburst. For a moment he kept silent, his brain struggling to cope with the amazing things he'd just heard; scared to speak in case he upset the Prof again.

But the Prof seemed to have calmed down. And there was something Ellis just *had* to know.

"Does Meriel remember what she did?" he asked the Prof. That would be a terrible burden to bear, to see the Prof's eyepatch and scarred face every day and think, *I did that.*

"She remembers some things about those days but not that," the Prof answered. "Not that she blinded me."

"Didn't she ever ask?" said Ellis. "I mean, how you got your injuries?" Ellis had asked once himself, but the Prof had just shrugged and said, "Oh, that's an old story."

"You know Meriel," said the Prof. "She's not curious about humans. Anyway, I never want her to find out." He looked pointedly at Ellis.

Ellis got the message. "Don't worry," he said. "I won't breathe a word."

The Prof nodded, as if he was satisfied. Then he went on with his story.

"Anyway, I managed to get hold of Meriel. She was clawing and biting and snarling. Then the mother dog sprang at me. I fell back over some rocks – that's when I hurt my leg. But I never even felt it until later. I kept tight hold of Meriel but the dog came after me. She leaped for my throat."

"So what did you do?" Ellis burst out.

"I stuck my arm down the dog's throat," said the

Prof. "I had to, to stop her killing me." He rolled up his right sleeve. The Prof always wore long sleeves – now Ellis knew why. His right arm was covered in thick ropey scars where the flesh had been torn.

"The dog's teeth did that," said the Prof, shrugging as if it was no big deal. "But she had to let go, she was choking. That gave me time to get Meriel into the canoe and paddle away. Later on, I passed out and some fishermen found us, drifting..."

The Prof paused. He sighed and looked at Ellis. "I sometimes wonder if I did the right thing."

"What do you mean?" asked Ellis.

"I mean, taking Meriel away from her wild dog family, bringing her back here to the city. As we paddled away, she howled at them across the water – these terrible, heart-rending howls. And they howled back. Until they were too far away to hear each other. Then she crumpled up in the bottom of the canoe and cried as if her heart was broken."

"Course you did the right thing!" said Ellis. "What else were you supposed to do? Leave her there?"

The Prof shook his head. His gaze, that had been far away in the past, seemed to snap back to the present. "No, of course not," he said briskly. "You're right. What else could I have done?" But he still seemed uncertain.

Ellis gave the Prof a sudden sharp stare. "Is that what you meant about good memories? Do you think Meriel sometimes wishes she was back there? With the dogs instead of with us?"

"I hope she doesn't," said the Prof. "But she might do, sometimes. You never know with Meriel."

"You never know with Meriel," repeated Ellis. But he wasn't really aware what he was saying. He was too busy trying to get his head round what he'd just been told. He'd always known the Prof and Meriel were close. Now he knew why.

The Prof rolled down his sleeve, covering the scars. "Well," he said, "now you know why Meriel's so anxious to go on this mission. Because this wild boy reminds her of herself. And you can see why I'm so worried. It's a minefield of memories for her – I don't know how she's going to react."

Ellis said, "You think she'll remember what really happened? How it was because of her that you lost your eye?"

"I don't know," said the Prof. "But one thing's for

certain. There's absolutely no way we can stop her going."

"No way," echoed Ellis. If they tried, Meriel would take off on her own. She was determined to find that boy before anyone else did.

Does JJ have any idea what he's done? thought Ellis, grimly. The forest would be full of people now, trying to catch the wild boy. JJ probably wanted to pose with him for a front page picture.

"This wild kid," said Ellis. "When we've found him, what should we do with him."

The Prof frowned. "I've been thinking about that. He needs special care. It might be best to let the child experts take him—"

"That's not what you did with Meriel," Ellis interrupted.

"*Shh!*" the Prof warned him. "She's back."

Meriel burst into the kitchen, carrying one tiny backpack. "I'm ready," she said, shrugging it on. "Come on, Ellis, shift your lazy butt." She dashed out of the kitchen, her long hair flying.

"Wait a minute, Meriel!" the Prof called after her. "Forest Edge is over three hundred kilometres away. Just how are you planning to get there?"

"By plane is quickest," said Ellis. "It takes less than two hours – provided there's no bad weather," he added. Just remembering yesterday's nightmare flight made him feel queasy.

"Phone JJ," ordered Meriel impatiently, poking her head back into the kitchen. "Make him send his dad's plane."

"No way!" said Ellis. "I'm not asking JJ for any favours!"

"You don't have to," said Prof. Talltrees, picking up the phone. These days the Prof didn't go out much; he mostly stayed in his lab studying dinosaurs. But it was amazing how many people he knew. He had contacts all over the world from his travelling days.

"I've got an old friend who owns an aeroplane," he explained. "I'm sure if I asked him, he'd fly you up there."

Chapter Six

This time, there were no storms. The little plane, with the Prof's friend at the controls, was flying north to Forest Edge through a clear blue sky.

"We'll land in the same place I did last night," Ellis told Meriel. "We'll be there by 4 o'clock. That gives us a few hours of daylight."

But if the search took longer than that it was no big deal. He and Meriel could live outdoors for weeks if they had to. Ellis had learned survival skills in Africa – he could make fires, build shelters. And Meriel could mind-read wild creatures to find the nearest food and water.

Ellis was a bit worried about that freaky weather though. If the temperature dropped way below zero, like it had last night, even he and Meriel might have to turn back. *It won't happen again*, he reassured himself. *It was just a one-off. Maybe something to do with that storm.*

"We should head straight for the lake," he told Meriel. "That's where I saw the wild boy – and Star. I think I saw a cave, too. Maybe that's where he lives with his greyhounds. Don't you think it's amazing, the way he saved their lives?" Ellis gave a low whistle. "If Hunter knew, he'd go ballistic!"

"A cave," murmured Meriel. "I lived in a cave once."

"What?" Ellis turned to stare at her. Her eyes had gone all dreamy. She'd been talking to herself, not to him. *What's going on in her head?* Ellis asked himself. *What is she remembering?*

But he didn't dare ask her. That might stir up bad memories. Memories that should stay buried – like how she injured the Prof.

"In a cave," whispered Meriel again.

Usually Meriel had no time for the past. She lived in the present, like animals do. But old, unsettling memories were surfacing – memories of when she lived with dogs, before the Prof found her and brought her back to civilization.

The memories seemed so real, it could have been yesterday. She was wriggling in a nest of puppies. She could smell their warm doggy smell. Now they were play fighting, nipping each other but not hurting, rolling about in the grass. Meriel gave some small, soft yelps, which no one heard above the noise of the plane engine.

She felt herself being carried, from one cave to another, gently, in the mother dog's jaws. Strapped into her plane seat, Meriel smiled.

And along with these vivid pictures, one word floated into her mind. It was "happy".

There'd been no confusion then; she'd known for certain where she belonged.

"I wish we'd get there!" said Meriel, twisting about in her seat. "I want to be there, now, this minute."

* * *

While Ellis and Meriel were flying to the forest, the Prof was doing some detective work. Who was this mysterious wild boy? He wanted to find out.

The Prof already knew a lot about feral children. After he'd found Meriel, he'd researched the subject. Often, they were runaways, from cruel families. Sometimes from care homes. That made him think about the dog collar Ellis had found in the forest and the address on its metal tag – *Forest Edge Children's Care Home*. Was it a clue? It might have no connection at all with the wild boy, but it was a place to start.

At first the Prof thought it was a dead end; after a few phone calls, he found out that the care home had been closed three years ago. He made more phone calls, trying to find out about the people who'd worked there. And eventually, someone told him about Mr. Leon Stubbins.

"He's the guy you need," they told the Prof. "He was the cook there for more than forty years. He's in an old folks' home now, though. I don't know how sharp his mind is."

So Professor Talltrees called the old folks' home. The phone rang and rang. But there was no answer.

Suddenly the Prof caught sight of the television news. It was from Forest Edge again. A great hulking guy in combat gear was on the screen. He had a net slung over his shoulder, a hunting knife stuck in his belt. The camera swung to JJ, who looked tiny beside him. The Prof turned up the sound.

JJ said, "*The Forest Edge Echo* is very concerned for the welfare of this feral child. So it has hired Mr. Hunter to catch him. Can you do the job, Mr. Hunter?"

"I'll bring the wild kid out," growled Hunter. "Don't you worry. And don't anyone else bother trying. Because they'll only get in my way."

JJ was right. Hunter was a menacing guy. The Prof swore softly to himself. He was seriously worried at this latest development. It meant danger, both for his wards and the wild boy.

He tried the old folks' home again. This time, a woman answered. He asked to speak to Mr. Stubbins. The woman said, "I'll take the phone through to him. He's just woken up from his afternoon nap."

The Prof and Leon had a long, long telephone conversation.

When it was over, the Prof put down the phone, very slowly. He sat for a moment, stunned.

He knew now who the wild boy was. He was a boy called Blue, who'd run off from the Forest Edge Care Home five years ago with an old, sick dog named Tyson. Neither he nor the dog had ever been seen again.

And Leon had told him some really alarming things about this runaway.

According to Leon, Blue wasn't a poor harmless boy. He had incredible powers. And he'd used them to kill people.

"The matron froze to death!" Leon had said. "Right in the middle of summer! No one could ever explain that. But I could. I saw Blue do it. I never told on him though. I never told the police, or anyone. That matron was a cruel, cruel woman. And besides, I liked the boy."

The poor guy's old, he's mixed up, thought the Prof. Leon couldn't have seen Blue do that. It just wasn't scientifically possible.

But, on the other hand, Leon hadn't sounded like a muddled old man. He'd sounded bright and alert.

"I can't believe Blue might be still alive," he'd said. "We thought he'd drowned, when we found his clothes on the riverbank. Take my advice, mister

– if it is Blue, he's better left in the forest. Don't go looking for him. He's like some kind of lethal weapon!"

The Prof phoned Ellis's mobile. A faint voice answered, "Hi, Prof."

"Hunter's coming into the forest," said the Prof. "JJ hired him to catch the wild boy."

Ellis's voice came again, even fainter now. "That creep JJ—!"

"And listen, Ellis," interrupted the Prof, "there's another thing. I think I know who the wild boy is. His name is Blue and I know this sounds totally ludicrous but... Ellis are you there?"

"Did you say Blue? That's a weird name..."

"Ellis, you're breaking up!"

There was a long beep. Then silence. The Prof tried to call Ellis again but couldn't make contact.

The Prof rubbed savagely at his scars. He never went with Ellis and Meriel – his lame leg would only slow them down. But this time was different. He had a very bad feeling about this mission.

He went to his study, switched on his computer. He googled a map of the Forest Edge area and studied it. A river ran past the town and right through the forest. If you turned off it, into a stream, it took you right to the lake, where his wards were headed.

"Wonder if you could get a small boat all the way?" the Prof asked himself.

He went limping out of his study. He was going down to the basement, to see if his old canoe was still in good working order.

Chapter Seven

Ellis put away his mobile. "It's useless. The signal's gone."

"What did the Prof say?" asked Meriel.

"He said Hunter's coming into the forest to catch the wild boy. I can't believe it," said Ellis, angrily. "You know what JJ did? He's supposed to be bringing the guy to justice for dog poisoning. Instead, he goes and hires him!"

"Then we've got to hurry," said Meriel. "Find the wild boy before Hunter."

"Oh, and the Prof said something else. He said the wild boy's name is Blue."

"Blue?" said Meriel. "How's he know that?"

"I don't know. We got cut off."

The plane that had brought them here was taking off again. It soared into the sky. The pilot waved. To him, they looked very small and alone down there. The vast forest, that spread from the far horizon, seemed about to sweep over them, like a dark sea.

"Maybe if I walk over there," said Ellis, waving his arm towards the town of Forest Edge, "I could get a signal. Call the Prof back."

"What for?" said Meriel. "We got his warning, didn't we, about Hunter? So let's go."

They sneaked past Hunter's shack. There were no signs of life. Had he already started out to search for Blue?

Meriel gave the shack a contemptuous glance. "Dog poisoner," she spat out, her eyes flashing.

"Watch out for his booby traps," whispered Ellis. But he didn't need to warn Meriel. She stood, quivering like an animal, before the pitfall trap. She seemed to know, instinctively that, if she took another step, she'd plunge through the grass into the deep hole beneath.

"There's a spring trap, too," said Ellis, walking carefully around it. Meriel tripped it, by kicking away the peg, as she passed. The willow swooshed up into the air, with the noose dangling harmlessly. "Ha!" she snorted. "That's spoiled his trap!"

At least the deadfall trap wasn't dangerous. Hunter hadn't had time to reset it – the boulder still lay where it had crashed down.

Ellis stopped for a second to study it. He had to give some credit to Hunter. He might look like a big, dumb brute, but it would be stupid to underestimate him. When it came to catching animals, or people, he was an expert.

Ellis suddenly realized Meriel wasn't beside him. She'd whisked into the trees without him.

"Meriel!" he shouted, breaking into a run. "Wait for me!"

Meriel flew along the forest tracks. Her feet seemed to have wings. Finally she stopped, gazed around her at the tall green pines, creaking and whispering in the wind.

I'm lost, she thought. But it didn't worry her. She'd meet up with Ellis at the lake. But which way was it?

She told herself, *Find Blue's dogs.*

Wherever his dogs were, the wild boy would be with them. And there was a strange, longing ache in her heart – she wanted to be there too. She was mad with impatience; she just couldn't wait.

She took off again, leaving Ellis even further behind.

"Yowwwwl!"

Meriel heard a faint howling from deep in the forest. Was that one of the wild boy's family?

She turned her face in that direction. And, suddenly, without even thinking about it, she threw back her head. The eerie sound that came out of her own throat surprised her.

"Yoowwwwl!" It was a long, answering call, like a lonely wolf, howling at the moon.

Didn't know I could do that, thought Meriel, impressed. She thought she'd forgotten that old dog language.

The other dog howled again, leading her on. It thought she was another greyhound. It was guiding her to the lake. With a happy smile on her face, Meriel followed its calls, pausing every now and then to throw back her head and let rip with an answering howl that meant, *I heard you! I'm on my way!*

She stopped for a moment. Could she mind-read the dog who was calling to her? Usually, she had to see the creature she was mind-reading – that's when it worked best. But sometimes, even without seeing the animal, she could pick up its mind vibes. It was a bit like tuning in to the right radio station. The distant dog howled again. Meriel screwed her eyes tight shut and concentrated fiercely on its voice.

And suddenly, *wham*, there she was, right where she wanted to be, inside the dog's head, feeling what it felt, seeing the world through its eyes.

She was panting, hot, she could feel her long tongue rolling out. It lapped up cold, sparkling water. Now she was sniffing, nosing among red and yellow flowers...

"Ohhhh." Meriel sighed with disappointment.

Her eyes shot open. She was back in her own skin – it had been all too short a visit. But her mind-reading skills were like that. Sometimes they worked okay. Sometimes they were so uncontrollable, they scared her stiff.

But the dog whose mind she'd just left was calling again, more urgently this time, as if to say, *Where are you? We're waiting. Get a move on.*

Meriel howled back and hurried deeper into the forest. She was getting really excited. The howls were louder now; the lake couldn't be far.

But something was puzzling her, too. Just now, when she'd been in that greyhound's head, something hadn't been right. She struggled to figure it out. That was another unpredictable thing – sometimes she could remember her mind-reading trips perfectly. Every detail was vivid and clear. Sometimes she could only remember fragments and sometimes, nothing at all.

But this time, she *did* remember.

I saw red and yellow flowers, she thought, amazed.

If she'd been seeing through a greyhound's eyes, she couldn't have seen that. Dogs have limited colour vision – they can't tell the difference between red and yellow. To them, both of those colours look the same.

Then it hit her, like a bombshell. "I wasn't in a dog's mind. I was in *his* mind, Blue's!"

It was Blue who'd been lapping up river water on all fours, sniffing at the pongiest smells. It was *his* howls she'd heard. He was calling to her now, through the forest.

Nothing much surprised Meriel. But she was astonished now. She'd never been able to read people's minds before. People's minds were too messy; they put up too many defences. So why could she read Blue's?

Because he's more animal than human, Meriel answered her own question. Sometimes, people had said the same thing about her – she always took it as a compliment.

Even more fascinated now, she rushed on. She didn't give a thought to Hunter – he didn't concern her. This was between her and Blue. She called to Blue in dog language and he called back. Between the trees, the golden pools of sunlight were changing to shadows. The sky overhead was tinged with pink. Before too long, the sun would be setting. But Meriel didn't notice.

Blue was barking now, short excited yelps. Meriel barked back. He was very close. She heard water tumbling. Was that a waterfall?

Then, suddenly, they met. She saw the blue glare of his eyes. Then the wild boy stepped out of the trees. It was just like Ellis had said. He had long tangled hair and was dressed in rabbit skins. His body was tanned deep brown and criss-crossed with scars and scratches. He had bare feet and thick, callused skin on his palms and knees where he'd run, on all fours, with his dog pack.

Blue was more shocked than Meriel. When he'd been calling to her, through the forest, he'd thought she was another dog. Maybe a stray that had wandered into the woods. It never occurred to him that she could be human. He hated humans. They'd tried to make him the same as them. But he wasn't a human, he was a dog.

He dropped onto all fours and bared his teeth, ground into sharp points from gnawing bones.

A dog slid out of the forest.

It's Star, thought Meriel immediately. Star was a

beautiful, brindled greyhound, just like Ellis's description.

Blue licked Star's face, as if to say, *We're family*.

Other greyhounds loped up and crowded round him, protectively. Low snarls rumbled in their throats.

"You're Blue, aren't you?" said Meriel.

Blue growled menacingly at her: "*Grrrr*."

Then his mouth gaped open like a red cave. He burst into a wild frenzy of barking. Foam speckled his lips.

Meriel flinched. But then she controlled herself and stood perfectly still. She knew a lot about predators – she'd been inside their minds often enough. She knew the slightest movement, or show of fear, would make the boy and his dogs attack her.

She didn't lower her head. Instead, she raised it, and made direct eye contact with Blue. She didn't use his human name again – he didn't seem to like that at all. Instead she fixed him with that intense, challenging stare that Ellis and the Prof knew so well.

Blue stopped barking.

He growled at her, but it was a hesitant growl. Meriel bared her teeth and growled back.

Blue could've frozen her to death, like he could any human who threatened him. But what was she? Dog or human? She spoke like a human. She called him a name he'd almost forgotten. But she spoke dog language too. And there was a wildness in her eyes he recognized.

Blue stared at her, puzzled, fascinated, scared – all the time making little whimpering noises. He didn't know how to deal with her.

So he just ignored her. He turned his back, dropped onto all fours and trotted with his dog family back to their cave behind the waterfall, hoping she'd go away.

But Meriel didn't go away. She glanced back once over her shoulder, as if to the human world she'd left behind. Then she dropped onto all fours and followed them.

Meanwhile, Ellis was following Meriel's tracks. He knew she was getting further ahead. He'd heard howling, too, from somewhere deep in the forest. An eerie howling that made his skin crawl.

At first, the tracks wandered about, went in

circles. Ellis thought, *She should have waited for me. She's lost.*

He kept an eye out for Hunter, but he didn't see him. Ellis wasn't too concerned about Meriel: she could take care of herself. But Blue seemed so small and skinny, so defenceless. If Blue had to be captured, Ellis didn't want Hunter to do it.

Hunter might hurt him, Ellis worried.

Besides, Hunter should be punished for dog poisoning, not made into a hero for catching some poor, harmless wild boy.

Now Meriel's footprints had become a scuffled blur. *She must have stopped here. Why?* wondered Ellis.

Then she'd set off again. But now her footsteps were different. They were purposeful, confident.

She's heading straight for the lake, thought Ellis.

From the heart of the forest came more howling. Ellis shivered. Then he reminded himself, *They're not ghost dogs. They're real.* Blue had saved all their lives, when Hunter had left them for dead.

What would happen, wondered Ellis, if Blue was brought back to civilization and looked after by child experts? Would they let him see his dogs?

I bet they won't, thought Ellis. *I bet they never let him see them again.*

But didn't the child experts know what was best for him? The Prof said, "Blue needs their care." While Meriel said, "What do *they* know?" Ellis shook his head in confusion. He didn't know who was right, the Prof or Meriel. He respected them both in different ways – he didn't want to have to choose between them.

He concentrated again on Meriel's tracks. She was running like a hare. He'd have to move faster if he wanted to catch up. She'd probably reached the lake by now. But tracking takes time. If you hurry you miss things, make mistakes.

Ellis wondered what would happen when Meriel met Blue. *Wow!* he thought. *Two wild kids together!*

He remembered Meriel's past and had a sudden twinge of anxiety. Did Meriel really wish that she was back with her family of wild dogs?

Naa, Ellis tried to reassure himself. *Course she doesn't. That's ridiculous.*

And there was the other worry, too. Would she remember that the Prof was badly scarred and half blind because of her?

Don't know if I could handle that, thought Ellis, *if I suddenly remembered. Even if I'd only been little. Even if it wasn't my fault.*

Suddenly he gasped, "Oh no!" and dropped belly-down into the grass. He'd seen another footprint. It was Hunter's combat boot.

Still lying flat, Ellis studied Hunter's tracks. They weren't from last night. They were fresh, made in the last fifteen minutes. The crushed grass hadn't even sprung back yet. And Hunter seemed to have picked up Meriel's trail. She didn't know it, but she could be leading him straight to Blue.

Ellis's mind raced for a minute. How could he distract Hunter, throw him off the scent?

Suddenly he thought of a way. What if he pretended to be the wild boy? Lured Hunter away from Blue and Meriel? It was risky, *very* risky. But it might work.

Grim-faced, Ellis took off his shoes and socks. He shoved them into his backpack and hid that under a bush. He smudged mud all over his face and clothes for camouflage, mussed up his hair. At the last minute he took off his watch – wild boys don't wear watches – and left that in his backpack, too.

Then he began to stalk Hunter.

Ellis flitted through the forest, making no noise. Gift, his African teacher, called this "the leopard walk" because leopards stalk you so silently. You don't even know they're there until you see the flash of their golden eyes. But by then it's far too late.

Ellis frowned. It was a bad idea, thinking about Africa. Next thing you knew, he'd be thinking about his mum and dad. And here came those painful memories, swamping him...

There was a sudden dry snap. He'd stepped on a twig. He cursed his own clumsiness, his lack of concentration.

Ahead of him, something moved in the shadows. A dark shape was hurrying this way.

Hunter! thought Ellis. *He's heard me!*

He crouched down and froze. If you stayed absolutely still, like a rock, you became invisible. He'd learned that from Gift. And sure enough, Ellis saw Hunter's gaze pass over him, as if he wasn't there.

As soon as he heard Hunter walking on, Ellis moved too. He took off again, making a wide sweep around Hunter through the forest.

He came out just ahead of him. He could hear

him, smashing through the bracken, coming this way, following Meriel's trail. Ellis chose a muddy spot, right on Hunter's path. Quickly, he stamped in it, pressing his bare feet firmly into the mud. Then he dropped on all fours and added some handprints. You'd have to be blind not to see them.

Then Ellis shrank back into the bracken and waited to see what Hunter would do. He came stomping up with his big knife stuck in his belt and the net slung over his shoulder.

Hope he's not used to tracking people, thought Ellis.

Anyone trained to track people would know immediately that they weren't the prints of a wild boy. A boy who walked barefoot all the time would have tough, callused feet. He'd have grippy toes, too, more like a gorilla than a kid. There'd be a hundred differences from someone who usually wore shoes.

But Hunter didn't know any of this. Or maybe he was only thinking about the money JJ had promised him. He stooped to look quickly at the prints, then straightened up with a whoop of triumph.

That's when Ellis made his move. He waggled

the bracken above his head.

"Hey, wild kid!" yelled Hunter. "That you?"

Ellis dashed through the bracken, not walking like a leopard this time, but making as much noise as he could.

"Come over here!" shouted Hunter. "I'm not going to hurt you!"

Ellis broke cover. He scuttled from the bracken to the nearest pine tree, making sure he left big, clear prints in the pine needles.

He crouched, panting, behind the tree, looking frantically round for his next cover. It was getting dark in the forest. That was good. Ellis didn't want to be seen too clearly.

Hunter was clumping behind him, crashing through bushes.

"Hey, little savage!" he yelled. "Might as well give up now! Don't you know it's me, Hunter, tracking you down?"

Ellis took a deep breath. He shot into the bushes again, making sure he broke a few twigs so Hunter could follow. Ellis was playing a deadly game of cat and mouse. At the moment, he was winning. But how long would his luck hold out?

Chapter Eight

Meriel was in the cave watching the greyhounds. She didn't stand up or make any sudden movements. She kept low, crouching, crawling, so the dogs wouldn't think she was a threat.

Outside, roaring water arched over the cave entrance. It sparkled red in the rays of the setting sun. But there was enough space behind the waterfall to slip into the cave. If you were quick, you didn't even get wet.

Inside, the cave was huge. It seemed as big as a cathedral, its roof lost in darkness. And there were greyhounds everywhere; young dogs, older dogs, even a few puppies, born here in the cave.

How many greyhounds? Meriel wondered, amazed. She lost count at twenty.

Blue had disappeared somewhere, into the cave's shadowy depths. Meriel was all alone with his dog family. She didn't know if she was welcome or not because, apart from one or two curious looks, she was being ignored.

The dogs went about their business – sleeping curled into balls, crunching on rabbit bones, sniffing each other, licking their puppies clean with raspy tongues.

Meriel wasn't a patient person. But, *Don't rush it!* she warned herself. She knew that you can't force yourself on animals. You have to respect them. They'll come to you if they want to – any friendship must be on their terms.

The cave was cosy and dry, with a sandy floor. It also stank with a rank, doggy smell. There was rotting meat, puppy poo around. But Meriel didn't mind that. And as she waited, she didn't feel scared at all. She felt a strange kind of inner peace.

She understood the rules here. Often the human world bewildered her. It seemed so complicated, so full of rules she didn't understand. She was always upsetting people, getting things wrong. It was much simpler with animals. They'd either accept her, or they wouldn't.

A pure white greyhound came loping up, on long slender legs. He was bigger than the others. He took a sniff at her, then drew back.

"*Grrr!*" he growled and bared his teeth. He could bite her, hurt her badly. But Meriel kept very, very still. She didn't run, because she knew he'd chase her. And even she couldn't outrun a greyhound.

"*Grrr!*"

Suddenly more growling came from the shadows. Blue shot out. He came scuttling over on his hands and knees, and placed himself between Meriel and the white dog. He bared his teeth too, protecting her. The white dog backed off and Blue seemed to lose interest in her. He went off to play fight with a puppy. They rolled over the cave floor, yelping and gently nipping each other.

Meriel watched them and waited, a quivering deep in her stomach.

Star came up. She sniffed Meriel all over. She shoved at her with a wet nose. Then, suddenly she licked Meriel's face, as if she was a puppy.

She trotted off. Meriel waited, hardly daring to breathe. Star came trotting back with a piece of gnawed rabbit skin in her jaws. It still had a few shreds of meat on. She dropped it before Meriel.

Meriel yelped, *"Yip, yip, yip."* That meant thank you. She picked up the rabbit skin and chewed at it.

Happiness flooded through her. She'd been accepted into the family.

Then disturbing thoughts flashed into her mind. *Where's Ellis got to? What if Hunter shows up?*

But, somehow, she just couldn't get worked up about it. Hunter, and even Ellis, seemed to belong to another world. A world that had nothing to do with her. That felt more and more hazy and far away.

Later, Meriel was having a drink in the warm summer evening. She was with Star, on her hands and knees, lapping water. Fireflies rose and fell over the surface of the lake.

Star sprawled out on a mossy ledge and Meriel lay beside her, with her head resting on Star's flank. She remembered doing this with her wild dog mother. She felt like a baby again, safe and happy and protected.

As the moon rose and turned the lake silver it seemed to her like a magical place.

I wish I could stay here for ever, Meriel thought.

She buried her nose in Star's warm fur. Dim memories came back, from a long time ago, from even before her dog family. They were of another mother, a human one this time, whose long, soft hair she'd cuddled into when she was very tiny. She could still remember its fragrant smell.

Meriel shook off the memory. It unsettled her. She was part of this dog family now. She didn't need a human one.

Later still, back in the dark cave, Meriel lay awake. Around her the greyhounds were peacefully sleeping. Blue was curled up, in a tangle of dogs, twitching and dreaming. He scratched madly at his fleas with a clawed hand, then settled down again.

Meriel wondered suddenly, *What's he dreaming about?*

Was it catching rabbits, or play fighting with puppies? Or scent marking trees.

Meriel smiled. *Bet it's something like that*, she thought. And she couldn't help herself – as he lay dreaming, she went into his mind.

Minutes later, she jerked out of her trance. She was shaking and sweating. What had she done that for? Blue's mind wasn't a happy dog's mind – she'd found horrors in there!

She tried to piece the pictures together. There'd been a woman with a fierce face, yelling. Then the woman's face changed to an icy mask, her eyelashes frozen together, her lips frosty blue, her teeth chattering...

"What's it mean?" Meriel whispered, her human speech sounding alien among the dogs' whimpers and snores. For a moment, she felt very alone. She wished she could ask Ellis or the Prof.

It was a long time before she could put those awful images out of her mind and fall asleep, like the rest of her new dog family.

Chapter Nine

Ellis was hiding in the bracken. He felt dizzy from exhaustion. His feet were cut and bleeding.

Where's Hunter? thought Ellis. His eyes flickered around. The forest was dancing with moonlight and shadows. Above him, the night sky was navy blue. A shooting star suddenly fizzed across it, like a firework.

He wondered what time it was. He seemed to

have been playing decoy for hours. He lifted his wrist to check his watch, then remembered that he'd left it behind.

You can't hold out much longer, Ellis told himself.

He'd led Hunter as far away as he could from the lake. He'd gained Meriel time, hours of it. Surely she must have found Blue by now?

It had been Ellis's plan to shake off Hunter, then join Meriel at the lake. But that wasn't proving to be easy. Hunter was like the Terminator. You couldn't escape him – he just kept coming.

And now, instead of luring Hunter on, Ellis was running ahead of him like a hunted creature, leaving bloody footprints behind him.

"Hey, wild boy!" came a taunting voice. It sounded totally confident and in control, as if Hunter was sure of getting his quarry.

Ellis ducked as the beam from Hunter's flashlight swept over his hiding place.

"Oh no!" he breathed. The beam swept back and made his shiny belt buckle flash.

Ellis took off again, in a crouching run. He was furious with himself: *You're getting careless!* The mud he'd smeared the buckle with had rubbed off somewhere.

His wobbly legs couldn't go much further. He just wanted to lie down and sleep.

Concentrate! Ellis told himself fiercely. Instead of just running, he needed to use his brain, to think of a way to lose Hunter.

The trouble was, he was too tired to think straight. His reactions were slow. His body ached all over and stung from scratches. His clothes were torn. And he was desperately thirsty. He crouched down and lapped water from a muddy puddle. His mind drifted again. At least it wasn't freezing like last night when ice sheets spread over the water and his fingers turned blue—

With a sickening shock, Ellis felt something grab his hair. He yelled, swivelled his eyes upwards.

Hunter was right above him, grinning down! He was lying stretched like a snake along a tree branch. He'd reached down, grabbed two handfuls of Ellis's hair, and now he was lifting him up by it, nearly ripping it out by the roots. Ellis yelled out with pain as he was hauled clean off the ground, his feet kicking helplessly, his fists flailing around.

Hunter got a better grip, on Ellis's shoulders. In a blind panic, Ellis wrenched his neck round and bit Hunter on the wrist, sank his teeth right in.

Hunter screamed, "You little...!" and dropped him.

Ellis was off again, diving into the bracken, tunnelling through it like a rabbit. How had Hunter done that? A big guy like him, sneaking up so silently, sliding out along that branch?

Told you not to underestimate him, flashed through Ellis's mind as he ran. He'd got arrogant, thought he could easily outwit a redneck like Hunter. And now he was learning humility the hard way.

He huddled, shivering, in his next hiding place. His ears strained, listening out for the sounds of Hunter stalking him, or his mocking voice: "Hey, wild kid. I'm coming to get you!"

Ellis needed to sleep so badly. His mind kept drifting off – he was almost hallucinating.

The Prof had told him once about Apaches – how the Native American warriors had sneaked up on the cavalry. There was no cover, just an empty grassy plain. When the cavalry scouts had checked it out, all they'd seen was open ground, scattered with big boulders. No chance of an ambush there! So the soldiers had ridden across it. Suddenly all those boulders had leaped up, whooping, and attacked them.

So stay still, Ellis told himself. *Like an Apache.*

It had worked before – Hunter had thought he was part of the scenery. But now Ellis couldn't control his body. It was trembling so much with weakness he was shaking the ferns.

But where was Hunter? He'd been quiet a long time.

Ellis saw two gleaming eyes. His heart almost stopped. Then he smelled a strong, musky stink. And he knew it was a fox slinking up to investigate. Perhaps it thought there was a sick rabbit in the ferns – easy prey.

"*Shoo*," hissed Ellis. The fox streaked off. But it was too late – Ellis was caught in the glare of a flashlight. He crashed through the undergrowth, away from the blinding beam.

In the next few seconds, he knew he'd been conned. Hunter wasn't where his flashlight was. And spread out in front of Ellis was a net.

Ellis could have swerved round it. But he didn't. He deliberately walked right into Hunter's trap, with his arms spread wide as if to say, *Okay, I give up*.

Ellis felt himself being swung up high.

"Gotcha!" he heard Hunter shout. "You little savage! You sure led me a dance!"

At first Ellis struggled. He couldn't help it; he hated cramped spaces. *I'm suffocating!* he thought, as the mesh tightened round him.

But then he was hoisted down and his face found holes in the net to breathe through. He calmed down, lay quietly and let his body go limp. At least he didn't have to run any more.

Dawn was breaking as Hunter strode out of the forest, with Ellis slung over his shoulder. In the grey, early morning light, a scrum of photographers and reporters was waiting.

"Here's your wild boy!" said Hunter triumphantly, spilling Ellis out of the net at their feet.

Ellis lay curled up on the ground, hiding his face. He was filthy, blood-streaked. His clothes were tattered. He looked totally defeated.

"Was he hard to catch?" asked a reporter.

"No problem at all," bragged Hunter.

"Look this way, wild kid!" yelled a photographer. There was a dazzling flash, as Ellis curled tighter into a ball. Over his head, reporters shouted questions.

"Stand back!" called a stern voice, used to giving orders. "Let the boy breathe!"

The crowd stopped yelling. There were no more blinding flashes. Cautiously, Ellis peeked through his fingers.

He saw a tanned, craggy face with steely eyes. He'd seen that face before on telly. It was Jay Harding Senior, the press baron, the man whose own son had to make an appointment to see him. And beside him stood JJ, leaning on his crutches, nervous, but glowing with pride.

"Told you Hunter would get him, Dad," he said. "Told you it'd make a great story."

Then, as he gazed at the huddled figure on the ground, JJ's voice suddenly filled with doubt.

"Wait a minute," he said. "This kid isn't dressed in rabbit skins."

Ellis uncurled himself and stood up. He was swaying a bit, but the fury he felt towards JJ had given him new energy.

"Hello, JJ," he said. "Remember me?"

"Hey!" yelled JJ. "What's happening here?"

He stared, bewildered, from Ellis to Hunter and back again.

"This isn't the wild boy!" he burst out. "I know this kid!"

There was a fresh clamour from the reporters, another frenzy of questions.

JJ Senior ignored them all. His flinty eyes were focused on his son.

"I'd like a word," he said to JJ, his voice somehow sounding more menacing because it was so soft and polite.

He pulled JJ and Ellis aside, away from the crowd.

"Is this some kind of hoax you've dreamed up with your friend here?" he asked JJ, furiously. "Does the wild boy really exist, or are you wasting my time?"

"No, Dad, it's no hoax," said JJ. He turned desperately to Ellis. "You've seen him, haven't you? Tell Dad that he's real."

It was Ellis's perfect chance. He should have said, "What wild boy? I haven't seen any wild boy." Then the hunt for Blue might have ended. And JJ would look like a prat.

Part of Ellis thought, *Serve him right.* He deserved it, after all the trouble he'd caused – telling lies, making himself out to be some kind of hero, turning the search for Blue into a media circus.

But, suddenly, Ellis couldn't do it. JJ was sixteen years old. But his face was crumpling like a little kid's as his dad turned his back, ready to stride away to his private jet.

"Wait, Dad," begged JJ. "Please, wait." Tears were streaming down his face. Ellis could hardly look. He felt so embarrassed and sorry for JJ he just couldn't handle it.

He suddenly blurted out, "JJ's right. That wild boy is real. I saw him at the lake."

He could have kicked himself. Why had he mentioned the lake? It had just slipped out somehow. He looked quickly over towards Hunter. Where was he? Shocked, Ellis realized that Hunter had sneaked up right behind them. He must have heard.

You and your big mouth! Ellis fumed at himself.

"See, I told you, Dad," JJ was saying, loudly. "Hunter just caught the wrong kid."

Some of the reporters started back to their cars. Others were laughing.

Hunter glared at Ellis. His eyes blazed with hatred and suspicion. "Nobody makes a fool of me," he growled. "I'll catch that wild kid if it's the last thing I do."

He came up very close to Ellis and hissed in his ear. "Don't know what your game is. But keep out of my way this time. The forest's a big place, accidents happen."

Collecting his net, he stomped away.

Ellis stared after him, his eyes clouded with worry.

Jay Harding Senior still didn't plan to stay. But his hard eyes had softened a little. "I've got a busy schedule today," he told JJ. "But call my secretary when you've got something. A feral child could still be big news. Good work, son."

JJ looked pathetically grateful. "I'll call you, Dad!" he shouted after him. "You can count on me!"

After his dad had gone, JJ stared at Ellis uneasily. He knew he had a lot of explaining to do. "Sorry," he shrugged. "I told a little lie – about breaking my ankle chasing the wild boy."

"A little lie!" said Ellis. He was going to add, "And what about hiring Hunter? You forgotten he poisoned those dogs? Or don't they matter any more?"

But suddenly he thought, *What's the point?* JJ couldn't be trusted. He'd do anything to please his dad – lie, cheat, break his promises.

So Ellis shrugged too. "Look, I haven't got time to talk. I'll see you later, JJ."

"Where are you going?" asked JJ, as Ellis stumbled off.

Ellis didn't even bother to reply. He had to beat Hunter to the lake. But his bare feet were bleeding; every step made him wince. First he needed to collect his hidden shoes. There were sandwiches and drink, too, in his backpack.

Ellis was about to plunge back into the forest. But suddenly a firm hand fell onto his shoulder. Panic shot through him. He whirled round. But it wasn't Hunter.

Ellis gazed up, amazed. "Professor Talltrees!" he gasped. "What are *you* doing here?"

Chapter Ten

A short time later, Ellis was sitting in the bow of the Prof's old canoe. They'd just pushed off from the rocky shore and were heading downriver, into the forest.

"Tell me what happened," said the Prof.

So Ellis told him, all about how Meriel had run into the forest ahead of him and how he'd pretended to be the wild boy to stop Hunter from following her straight to Blue.

"That was good work," said the Prof.

"Yeah, but it was all wasted," said Ellis bitterly. "Because I just went and opened my big mouth and now Hunter knows exactly where to find them."

"Don't worry," said the Prof. "With any luck we'll be at the lake before him."

"Have you brought any food?" asked Ellis. "I'm starving."

The Prof said, "Look in that dry bag tied under your seat. There's some food and water."

"Cool!" said Ellis.

Ellis unzipped the dry bag. The Prof had packed chocolate for energy and some dried fruit and nuts. Ellis wolfed down the lot, then took a big swig of water.

The Prof had driven through the night to reach Forest Edge, with his canoe on top of his car. He'd arrived just minutes after Hunter came swaggering out of the forest, with Ellis slung over his shoulder.

The Prof was steering from the stern, paddling with long easy strokes. He had sunglasses on, to protect his eye from the water's sparkling glare.

"Want me to paddle?" Ellis asked.

But the Prof said, "No, not until I tell you."

So there was nothing for Ellis to do but sit back and enjoy the ride, at least until they got to the lake. He needed the rest, after last night's frantic chase through the forest.

He inspected his feet. They were a mess – all cut and blistered.

"There are some spare clothes in the bag," said the Prof. "And a pair of old trainers and hiking socks."

Ellis rummaged in the dry bag again. He grinned as he found the Prof's telescopic walking stick. The Prof never used it unless he was forced to – he was too proud.

The Prof's spare trainers were way too big. But two pairs of thick hiking socks helped them fit, more or less.

Ellis took off his life jacket, changed his torn, dirty T-shirt. But he didn't need the extra sweaters the Prof had brought. The sun was burning off the early morning mist. Soon, it would be a really hot day. The freezing cold weather of the night before last, when he'd first seen Blue, seemed like a distant memory.

"Put your life jacket back on," the Prof told Ellis.

"Yeah, yeah," said Ellis, over his shoulder.

He thought a life jacket was a bit over-the-top, like the warm clothes the Prof had packed. The river was wide and calm as a pond. He could see fish glittering beneath the canoe, darting over the stones.

If I fell in there, thought Ellis, *it'd only come up to my knees.*

But then the Prof paddled out to the middle of the river. Instantly a strong current grabbed the light metal canoe, whisked it away. The Prof paddled faster. Now they were speeding along, over deep, green water.

Hey, thought Ellis, *this is a great way to travel!* And the scenery was pretty, like a picture postcard. On either side, pine-covered slopes swept right down to the riverbank. Behind them, rugged hills rose in the distance.

But then Ellis's mind went back to the mission. Meriel was probably with Blue right now. He wondered what was happening. And what Meriel was remembering, from her life with wild dogs.

"Did you find out anything else about Blue?" he asked the Prof. "I mean, apart from his name?"

The Prof was concentrating on paddling, switching sides from left to right, to keep the canoe in the current. But in a few short sentences, he told Ellis what he knew. That Blue had been abandoned at the care home when he was a baby. But five years ago he'd run off with Tyson the care home dog.

"Leon said poor old Tyson was on his last legs," added the Prof. "So that was obviously his grave you found."

Ellis thought about the pebble pyramid. Blue must have built that for Tyson, his old friend, and was still putting fresh flowers on it. It showed he wasn't just a savage child without any feelings.

"Blue really cared about that dog," said Ellis. "He must've been gutted when it died."

"But he soon found some more dog friends," said the Prof. "The greyhounds that Hunter tried to kill."

The Prof swatted some flies from his face. He paddled the canoe into a quiet pool, so he didn't have to shout above the rushing water. "There's one other thing. Leon said Blue had these amazing powers. That he could make the air temperature drop below freezing. Leon said, 'That boy could bring on winter just by looking.'"

Ellis's mouth fell open. The canoe rocked, as he swivelled round to face the Prof. "You're kidding! You're saying that it wasn't just freaky weather the other night? That Blue did it?"

"I'm not saying anything," said the Prof, "I'm just telling you what Leon told me. He said something else, too. He said Blue froze the matron of the care home to death. Deliberately. On a hot summer's day, just like this one."

Ellis stared at the Prof. He felt the hairs creep on the back of his neck. He burst out, "You don't believe that, do you? That's crazy!"

"I agree, it's crazy," said the Prof, rubbing at the scars that ran from under his eyepatch. "But, nevertheless, I won't be happy until we've found Meriel." He paddled them back into the current.

They were speeding along again, the Prof driving the canoe down the river with swift, strong strokes. But now Ellis wasn't appreciating the scenery – he was deep in his own thoughts.

"It's crazy," Ellis murmured again. But Leon's words echoed in his head. *He could bring on winter just by looking.* Ellis remembered Blue's pale frosty eyes; that icy stare that seemed to freeze the marrow in your bones.

And suddenly, he was desperately worried about Meriel, too. "How long until we get to the lake?" he asked the Prof.

The Prof didn't answer. He was busy avoiding a dead tree that had washed down the river and got stuck in some rocks. Its white branches waved above the water like ghostly arms.

"Strainers," said the Prof. "That's what canoeists call washed-up trees. They're the most dangerous thing on a river. Apart from rocks."

Ahead of them the river bent sharply left, and Ellis heard a rumbling, roaring sound, as if a monster was waiting round the corner. It got louder as the bend came nearer.

"Put your helmet on," instructed the Prof. He was already strapping his under his chin. He passed one forward to Ellis.

"Do I have to?" said Ellis.

"Just do it," said the Prof, urgently. "There's white water ahead. And pick up your paddle. But don't paddle until I tell you."

The canoe swept round the bend. Ellis gasped out loud. Sheer cliffs towered on both sides. And the river squeezed between them, a riot of racing, boiling foam. Clouds of spray rose above it, full of glittering rainbows.

Ellis had time for only one shocked look. Then the power of the current grabbed them. As Ellis clung to the sides, the canoe was rocked, spun round, then flung into the chaos. Ellis was drenched immediately, spray lashing his face.

The canoe spun around again, was tossed from wave to wave like a ping-pong ball. The Prof sat tall in the stern, fighting the river, watching for obstacles over Ellis's head. Hanging on grimly, Ellis half turned, snatched a glance. His guardian was just a blurred shape in the spray blizzard. Ellis could see his paddle flash as it rose and fell.

A jagged rock loomed up.

"Paddle, Ellis!" yelled the Prof.

Ellis gripped his paddle tightly, dug it again and again into the raging foam. He didn't have time to think. The river's roar deafened him, spray blinded him. The canoe bashed a rock, boomeranged off.

"Left! Left!" yelled the Prof. "Pull left!"

Ellis switched sides, put his head down, paddled harder. Great, sobbing breaths were ripped from his body. A wave of icy green water broke over him, clear as glass. The shock made him gasp out loud. The river boomed in his ears, driving everything out of his head but one feeling. It wasn't panic, but fury. It was as if the river was trying to stop them getting to Meriel.

"You're not going to win!" Ellis told the river, paddling like a maniac, as the Prof skilfully steered them from rapid to rapid.

Then, all at once, it ended. They were spat out from the gorge. The sheer cliff walls had vanished and on each side were gentle tree-covered slopes. The river was still swift, but wider again, not so wild.

"Yay!" cheered Ellis. "We're out!" He felt like they'd beaten the river.

"That was fun," said the Prof. And Ellis was startled to see that the usually grave-faced boffin was grinning like a little kid.

Then, "Hey!" yelled Ellis in alarm, clutching the sides of the canoe. It had suddenly rocked violently. It rocked again, rose on a great wave of water. The Prof shot a look behind them.

"Watch out! Strainer!" he yelled.

A huge, floating tree rushed past them – then jammed in rocks ahead, blocking their way through.

"Back paddle!" screamed the Prof. But it was too late. The canoe was going to hit.

"Jump! Jump for the tree!" yelled the Prof.

Ellis felt the canoe being sucked from beneath him. Like a flying squirrel he launched himself at the tree. Half in and half out of the water, he clung on while the canoe was whisked under the strainer and on down the river, flipping over and over. The current was trying to drag him down, too – he could feel the pull on his legs. Ellis hauled himself higher and wedged himself between two big branches, shivering uncontrollably. The river surged past below him. He was safe though, for the moment. But where was the Prof?

And then he saw him. The Prof hadn't jumped for the strainer. He was chasing his canoe, feet first, on his back, letting the river carry him. His red helmet bobbed in the churning foam. Somehow, he'd kept hold of his paddle. He held it high in the air so the current didn't snatch it.

The Prof hit a whirlpool. He went round and

round, as if he was in a washing machine. Then he got sucked down.

"Prof!" yelled Ellis. But then he saw the waving paddle and the red helmet bob up, further downstream.

From his perch in the tree, Ellis had a bird's-eye view. The canoe was stuck upside down in some rocks. The Prof caught up with it and flung himself at the rocks, clinging onto them like a monkey. He hauled himself out of the water, stood up and looked around. There was a safe spot by the bank, where the water was calm. The Prof flipped the canoe right side up, got in it and launched it off the rocks, pushing with his paddle. A few strong strokes and he was into quiet water near the bank. He waved his paddle back at Ellis. That meant, *I'm okay!* Then he clambered out onto the bank and pulled the canoe after him.

Great work, Prof, thought Ellis.

But Ellis was still stuck in a tree in the middle of the river. The bank was too far to leap to. And swimming in this raging torrent was impossible.

He was wondering what to do next when suddenly he heard wood cracking. The tree he was clinging to started to shudder. It was moving!

What do I do now? thought Ellis, panicking. Should he hang on? Or let go and jump, get swirled away in the river?

His wet hands were slipping. Below him, the white splintered branches shook. One snapped clean off, got whisked away downstream, tumbling over, crashing into rocks as it went.

Ellis stared after it and clung on tighter. He'd be mashed to bits in that current. The Prof was a skilful canoeist; he knew how to ride the river and get out alive. Ellis had paddled boats before, but never in wild water like this.

"Oh no," groaned Ellis, as the tree give another sickening shudder. The river was working it loose like a rotten tooth, trying to wrench it out of the rocks. Ellis wrapped his arms and legs tighter around a branch, as if that could save him.

A voice yelled from the bank. "Ellis! Look this way! I'm going to throw a rope! You've got to grab it!"

It was the Prof. He'd left the canoe and come limping back upstream.

A rope came snaking through the air and caught

on a tree branch just above his head. Ellis watched it, as if in a dream.

"Grab the rope, Ellis!" yelled the Prof.

The tree cracked again, moaning like a wounded beast.

"Ellis!" shouted the Prof. "You've got to let go of the tree!"

Ellis clung on tighter, terrified of letting go.

"Listen to me!" bawled the Prof, even more urgently. "Do as I tell you! Grab the rope. The rope, Ellis!"

Suddenly Ellis seemed to wake up. He reached above him, snatched the rope and slithered down to a lower branch. Then he looped the rope around his wrists twice and threw himself into the water.

Seconds after he jumped, the tree gave a groan. Then, with one last terrible cracking sound, it was jerked loose and swept away downstream.

Ellis felt himself being yanked through the water on the end of the rope.

His life jacket kept him on his back and buoyant, but it was a bumpy ride. His helmet banged off rocks. Waves broke over his face, making him choke and splutter. And his arms were almost wrenched from their sockets.

Now he was being hauled through shallow water, his back scraping on pebbles.

Then, all at once, the dragging stopped.

Ellis lay there for a moment, dazed, the breath knocked out of him. Then he opened his eyes. He was staring up at a clear blue sky. The Prof was kneeling on the bank. He was gasping for breath too. It had taken all his strength to haul Ellis ashore, fighting the power of the river, when every second it wanted to claim his ward and drown him, or crush him to death against rocks.

Ellis stumbled out of the river, water streaming off him. He was bruised all over. The rope had tightened around his wrists, cut into them. "Ouch, that hurts!" said Ellis, as he prised it loose.

He took off his helmet, and shook his hair like a wet dog.

"Thanks," he said to the Prof. The Prof nodded, unable to speak. "You okay?" asked Ellis anxiously, putting his hand on his guardian's shoulder.

"Never better," croaked the Prof. He staggered to his feet, grimacing with pain – his lame leg had taken a battering. Together he and Ellis went back to the canoe.

"Look at that!" said Ellis, awed. The metal canoe was dented all over as if someone had attacked it with a giant hammer.

The Prof slid it into the water and inspected the damage.

"It still floats!" said Ellis, amazed.

The Prof nodded. "She's a good old boat. She's still watertight. She'll get us to the lake."

Even the dry bag was still there, secured under the stern seat.

"We've lost a paddle though," Ellis pointed out.

"That's a nuisance," said the Prof. "But at least we've still got one."

"Then let's go!" said Ellis, jumping back in. "We've lost a lot of time. What if Hunter gets to the lake before us?"

The Prof paddled the canoe in silence. The river was peaceful now, just rippling gently by. The roaring, pounding water was behind them. They could even hear birdsong. Ellis's wet clothes were drying already, steaming in the hot sun. He sat slumped in the bow, almost dozing off.

Then the Prof said, suddenly, "We have to talk about Blue."

Ellis's head jerked up. "What?" He swivelled round on his seat to face the Prof.

"We need to talk about Blue before we get to the lake," the Prof repeated.

"It's not about him freezing people to death, is it?" said Ellis. "You said you didn't believe that."

"I don't," said the Prof. "Not until I get more proof. But it's not about that. It's about what we do when we find him."

"You said before about handing him over to the child experts. But you didn't mean that, did you? They'd really mess him up!"

The Prof stayed silent.

"And we can't let JJ get his hands on him," Ellis rushed on. "He'd be put on show, treated like a freak."

For Ellis, there was only one solution. "We'll just take Blue home with us," he said.

"I was afraid you'd say that," said the Prof. "That's why we need to talk about it. You see, Ellis, looking after a feral child isn't simple at all. They have huge problems—"

"Look, I know it won't be easy," Ellis butted in.

"But you did it with Meriel. You took her home. And she was living with dogs when you found her, just like Blue."

The Prof sighed. He didn't say how tough it had been raising Meriel. How he'd retired from public life and devoted himself to it. And how he still wasn't sure whether he'd been successful – or even whether it had been the right thing to do.

He just shook his head and said, "It's a massive responsibility. You've got no idea. And it may not be best for Blue..."

"Course it is!" said Ellis, eagerly. "And me and Meriel will help you. Don't you worry! We'll look after him."

The Prof had to smile. "You're a good boy, Ellis," he said. "Your heart's in the right place."

Ellis said, "So we're taking him home with us? Right?"

The Prof sighed again. He could see Ellis wasn't in the mood to listen. That he'd already made up his mind about what should happen to Blue.

"Maybe we should talk about this later," said the Prof. "Let's get to the lake first, see what the situation is."

* * *

As the Prof paddled towards the lake, Meriel was in the cave with her dog family. They were sheltering from the fierce midday sun.

Blue had made himself a little scoop in the sand. He was curled up in it, snoozing, his belly fat with rabbit meat. Meriel hadn't been into his mind again. She didn't dare. It might spoil this animal paradise she'd found.

She didn't want to think at all, especially about the human world she'd left behind.

There's nothing I want back there, she told herself. All of them in this cave had been harmed by the human world – Blue, the greyhounds and her.

The human world thinks you're a freak, Meriel reminded herself.

She'd never truly belonged there. But she felt she belonged here. Here you didn't have to worry. In this world, animal instincts were all you needed.

A lazy bluebottle buzzed up, landed on her hair. She shook it off. She whimpered, like a puppy. Immediately, Star came over and licked her face, lay down beside her. Meriel snuggled against her, sniffing at her warm fur.

Blue had woken up. He came trotting past them on all fours, a bloody, half-eaten rabbit carcase swinging from his jaws. Meriel yelped a greeting, yawned, stretched and trotted out after him, leaving the other dogs dozing. The bright waterfall spray dazzled her eyes after the dark cave.

As Blue and Meriel crouched together on a rock, sharing meat, neither of them had a clue that Hunter was watching. He'd just arrived and was hiding in the reeds on the lake shore.

Two of them! he thought, his eyes widening. No one had said anything about *two* wild kids. But two was even better.

He was still furious about last night's failure. He wanted revenge on those soft city reporters who'd mocked him. He could see himself now, striding back into Forest Edge with two wild kids slung over his shoulders.

That'll show 'em, he thought. *That'll wipe those sneery city grins off their faces.*

And there was another bonus. Two wild kids meant double the money.

But catching them would take cunning. By rushing in too fast, he could lose one of them, or even both. He had to take his time, make preparations. He checked out the wild kids again. They were playing now, having a tug of war with the rabbit skin. Hunter could hear their happy yelps. They seemed completely unaware that they were in any danger.

Hunter smiled, a wolfish grin. He didn't need to stay watching them. Those two kids looked completely at home here – they weren't going anywhere. Unless they spotted him, of course. And he didn't want that before he was ready. It'd be best to stay out of sight of the lake shore for a while. He slunk back into the forest. He was going to set some traps.

Chapter Eleven

Ellis and the Prof had turned off into a side stream. It wasn't white water, but it was still hard going. The Prof was paddling against the current now. "This stream flows out of the lake," he told Ellis. "It should take us straight there."

The Prof paddled round a bend.

Suddenly, Ellis heard a low roaring sound, like some kind of giant engine.

"That's the waterfall," said the Prof. "We've made it!"

A big lake opened up before them, among the pines. There was a waterfall at the far end, glittering in the brilliant sunshine.

As they moved out onto the open water, Ellis cried, "There's Meriel!"

The Prof gazed across the lake. There, on the shore near the waterfall, was his ward. She was crouched on a rock. She seemed to be eating something. What was it? It was hard to see from this distance.

"What's she eating?" the Prof asked Ellis, who had much sharper eyes than his.

Ellis stared for a few seconds. Then he said, startled, "It looks like a piece of meat. But it's *raw*, all bloody."

The Prof swayed, put a hand to his head. It was just like his first sight of Meriel, when she was two years old. He had a sudden dizzy sense of time rushing backwards. As if all those years, when he'd struggled so hard to bring her up, had been wiped out at a stroke and meant nothing.

"Blue's with her," said Ellis. "Look, there he is."

Blue came scuttling round the rock. As soon as he saw the canoe, with its two human intruders, his face became a mask of hate. He snarled. Ellis could see his bared teeth glinting. Meriel's head whipped round too. But even Ellis couldn't make out the expression in her eyes. Then she dropped her meat and ran on all fours back behind the waterfall, to the safety of the cave and her dog family.

That left Blue alone on the rock. He didn't run. Instead, he squatted, still and silent, like the statue of some savage little god.

He was staring straight at them. Ellis couldn't see his eyes – but he didn't need to. Those eyes, like icy blue crystals, were burned into his brain. Ellis shuddered. He felt a tightening, deep in his stomach. There was something so creepy about that wild boy. You could almost believe he really did have extraordinary powers.

The Prof had recovered from his shock and was paddling strongly across the lake.

They were halfway to the waterfall when a shadow fell across them. The Prof stopped paddling, glanced up. The sun had been scorching in a clear blue sky. But now dirty white clouds came rushing in, from all directions. They met over the lake, covered the sun. All you could see of it now was a dim, pale yellow disc.

Then something white and feathery came drifting down from the sky. It landed on the back of the Prof's hand. He stared at it.

At first, his astonished brain couldn't take it in. He licked his hand.

"It's a snowflake," he said.

Suddenly, they were in a mini blizzard. A wind rose, whipping up the lake's surface, rocking the canoe.

"Hang on!" said the Prof.

As Ellis gripped the canoe's sides, snowflakes were flung in his face. He was blinded; he spat them out.

Then, as suddenly as it had started the snowstorm stopped. The air was free of white flakes, the clouds were gone. The surface of the lake was calm again, like a huge mirror. Blue was still crouched on his rock. His gaze never left them.

"It's happening just like before," said Ellis, "when I was in the forest. It's Blue doing it. It must be! That guy you spoke to on the phone was right!"

The Prof didn't answer. He wanted to get them off this lake, as fast as possible. He dug his paddle in the water. The water wasn't clear green any more, it had turned opaque black. And the paddle blade didn't sweep cleanly through – it met resistance.

The Prof thought, *This is a joke. This isn't happening.*

The water was thickening, changing colour. The Prof knew what that meant.

"It can't be," he murmured. His hands were tingling. They felt numb and clumsy, and it was hard to keep a grip on the paddle.

He dug the paddle in again. This time, the treacly water tugged at it, dragged it from his cold fingers. The Prof watched appalled, as their only paddle drifted out of reach.

"We'll paddle with our hands," he told Ellis, urgently. They were within shouting distance of the shore – they might be able to make it.

But when the Prof dipped his hand into the water, he pulled it out quickly: "Ouch!" The water was thick and sludgy, like a milkshake, and so cold it burned his hand like fire.

Then the Prof heard something that chilled his blood even more. It was a distant murmuring, as if a million voices were whispering. The Prof had read about this but had never heard it before. It was the sound ice made, as it spread.

"I think the lake's freezing up," he told Ellis, astonished.

"It's Blue," said Ellis again. "It must be."

The Prof stared across at the wild boy, unmoving on his rock, a skinny filthy kid, dressed in rabbit skins. Did Blue really have that kind of power? To bring winter on, to make a lake freeze so quickly? The Prof had told Ellis he needed proof. But wasn't he seeing it now, with his own eyes? The trees round the lake shore were snow-dusted. But the wooded slopes further back were green. There, it was still summer.

The Prof shook his head. "This is stupid. It's just not scientifically possible."

But Ellis didn't need any more convincing. "I'm going to swim to the shore, make Blue stop!" He got up from his seat.

"Are you *crazy*?" said the Prof, forcing him back down. "You wouldn't last two minutes in that water.

The cold would stop your heart before you drowned. Look over there!"

Ellis looked. Ice was coming towards them.

With terrible swiftness, it snaked out in tentacles from the shore. Now there were sheets of it, floating round the canoe. Then the sheets joined up, the spaces filled in like a jigsaw puzzle. And suddenly the ice stopped its whispering. It had finished its work.

Appalled, the Prof gazed at the frosty white surface, that stretched all around them. Under normal circumstances, it should have taken hours for this lake to freeze. But, fast as a speeded-up film, it had just happened in minutes. And they were stuck in the middle.

The Prof gripped the canoe sides, tried to rock it free. But it wouldn't even move; the ice held it fast.

"We're trapped," said the Prof, as if he still found it hard to believe.

Ellis wouldn't believe it either. "No, we're not! We'll just walk across the ice." The shore wasn't that far away.

"Wait!" said the Prof. He knew something about ice – he'd once spent a year studying wolves in the Arctic.

He leaned over the side of the canoe and pressed the ice. It felt elastic under his fingers, like a trampoline. He knew instantly that it wouldn't hold their weight. If they stepped onto it, they'd plunge through, into the black depths beneath.

"We can't walk on it yet," said the Prof. "We've got to wait until it gets harder."

"This is stupid!" Ellis was furious. He couldn't believe they were so helpless. "Let us go!" he yelled over the ice at Blue.

The Prof heard Ellis's shout echo round the lake. "Let us go – go – go." And suddenly he realized that, instead of the waterfall roaring, there was a deep, sinister hush.

He gazed, horrified, at the waterfall. It was silent, solid. It had frozen too, into a glittering ice curtain. Great sparkling icicles hung from the cliff around it. It might have been pretty, a winter wonderland, if it hadn't been so deadly.

The Prof was shivering already. He thought, *What's that clacking sound?* Then he realized it was his own teeth, chattering. It was the first sign of hypothermia.

He knew Ellis hadn't grasped yet the real

seriousness of their situation. They were trapped in the middle of a frozen lake, in sub-zero temperatures. If that ice didn't hurry up and harden, they would freeze to death out here.

CHAPTER TWELVE

Inside the cave, Meriel felt the temperature plummet, saw the waterfall turn from a foaming torrent into a silent crystal curtain. The sudden change from summer to winter alarmed her. But her dog family didn't seem surprised. They just yawned and scratched and snuggled closer together for warmth.

Then she heard a human voice from outside. It was Ellis shouting, "Let us go!"

Meriel shook her head violently from side to side, her hair swishing, like a dog pestered by flies.

She heard Ellis shout again. "Meriel, where are you?"

Then the Prof added his plea. "Meriel, we need you!"

His voice sounded desperate. She crammed her hands over her ears so she couldn't hear. She curled up next to Star, screwed her eyes tight shut and buried her nose in her dog-mother's warm fur. That brought back happy memories, of that time, years ago, with her wild dog family.

But what was this other memory, raw and vivid, slamming into her brain. It concerned humans, not dogs. Inside her head, Meriel told it, *Go away!* But she couldn't stop it. It replayed like a film in her mind.

The Prof was holding onto her, hugging her to him. She fought like a mad dog. She raked his eye and face, barking, foam flying from her mouth. She had his blood under her nails. But, despite her ferocity, he held on, hugged her even tighter. As if, now he'd got her, nothing would make him give her up.

Why'd he take me with him? thought Meriel,

trying to figure it out. *When I hurt him like that? I'd have dumped me, I'd have left me on dog island.*

She'd never understand humans.

Star licked at her face, trying to get her attention. Meriel pushed her away, distracted.

"I'm busy," she told Star, in her human voice. Inside her head, she was trying to work things out, replaying that mind-blowing, brutal memory over and over again.

"Quit this now!" yelled Ellis at the top of his lungs.

But the big freeze-up didn't thaw. Still Blue sat on his rock, casting his powerful spell. Either he hadn't heard, or he didn't care.

"Do you know what you're doing? We could die out here!" yelled Ellis.

"*Die, die, die,*" echoed around the frozen lake.

But Blue didn't move a muscle; he didn't even seem to be shivering. And all the time his eerie eyes stayed fixed on the two humans, trapped in their small canoe, in the middle of the vast, glittering ice field that he'd created.

"No use asking him to stop," Ellis decided. "He

wants to kill us. Like he killed that woman at the care home."

But he tried Meriel's name again. Surely she'd help them? Maybe she could stop Blue if they couldn't.

"Meriel, stop messing about! Get out here, we need help!" bawled Ellis, his shouts ringing off the frozen lake.

But Meriel didn't come out of the cave. Had she chosen sides, abandoned them, decided to stay with Blue and his dogs? Ellis could hardly believe it. He and Meriel were a team. They'd been through so much together on so many missions.

Ellis made one last desperate appeal: *"Meriel!"* Still she didn't appear.

"Looks like we're on our own, Prof," said Ellis.

The Prof didn't seem surprised, as if it was something he'd almost expected. He was rummaging in the dry bag. He found two of his old sweaters and handed one to Ellis. They pulled them on over their still-damp clothes.

"Try to keep yourself warm," said the Prof, clapping his arms over his chest. "Keep your blood circulating."

"I can't stop shuddering," said Ellis. Great big spasms were shaking his body.

"That's a good sign," said the Prof, through chattering teeth.

It was when you stopped shaking you had to worry. Then hypothermia had really set in. It meant your heartbeat was slowing and your body was starting to shut down.

"Isn't that ice h-h-hard enough to walk on yet?" asked Ellis, through frozen lips. It was their only hope of escape.

The Prof tested it again. It flexed a little under his hand but it seemed firm enough. He wasn't at all sure about the rest of the lake though. "We should wait a bit longer," the Prof decided.

Ellis didn't say anything to that. The Prof stared at him, slumped on his seat. Suddenly, he leaped up, slapped Ellis's face. "Wake up!"

"What?" Ellis said, groggily. "Whatsamatter? What you hitting me for?"

"You were asleep," said the Prof. "You mustn't fall asleep. If you fall asleep, you're as good as dead. You could freeze solid, sitting upright in this canoe."

He could feel his own brain getting sluggish. He tried to think. He knew he could endure these low temperatures longer than Ellis. Ellis was much lighter and skinnier, with less body fat.

The Prof changed his mind about waiting. "We've got to get you out of this canoe," he told Ellis, urgently. "Right now."

The Prof cast his eye again over the ice between the boat and the shore. He was reading it like a map, trying to remember all he'd learned in the Arctic. In some parts it was pearly blue, more solid. That was good ice, it would bear Ellis's weight. Other patches were like dark stains. That was bad ice. If Ellis stepped there, it would crack and he would plunge straight through.

The Prof had read once that, if you're trapped under ice, the world above looks like a bright neon glow. And that's the last thing you see before your heart stops.

Stop thinking about that! the Prof told himself savagely. He had to stay calm, crush his feelings. It was his ward's only chance of survival.

The Prof fumbled in the dry bag with freezing hands, got out his metal walking stick, extended it.

"Here," he handed it to Ellis.

"What's that for?"

"You're going to use this to track your way back to shore, over the ice."

"What, just me? I'm not leaving you here!"

"The ice won't bear my weight."

"Then we'll stay here until it freezes harder."

"No," said the Prof. It was no time to mince words. "You'll be dead by then. I can survive much longer."

"I'll g-g-get help," said Ellis. "I'll s-s-save you."

"I know you will," said the Prof, turning away to hide the bleak look in his eyes.

Although he knew staying in the canoe would kill him, Ellis suddenly felt scared to leave it. The frozen lake looked so wide and empty. The shore seemed so far away.

"I've never tracked over ice," said Ellis. "I don't know anything about it."

"But I do," said the Prof. "Just listen to me and you'll be all right."

Ellis swung his legs over the side of the canoe and stood up on the ice. At first, he swayed and slithered. "Hey!" he shouted out alarmed. Then he steadied himself with the Prof's stick, got his balance back. He tried a few shuffling steps away from the canoe.

For a few panicky seconds, the Prof almost called Ellis back. He thought, *I don't know enough about ice.* Inuit trackers took a lifetime to learn their skills.

Then he told himself, *Get a grip!* His ward's life was in his hands. He would need all his concentration to guide Ellis safely to shore. *You can do it!* he told himself. As long as he didn't give in to the strange lethargy that was creeping over him. That was another sign of hypothermia.

Ellis was standing, wobbling, out on the ice. "What do I d-d-do now?"

He deliberately didn't look at Blue, the winter bringer, still squatting on his rock. Was the wild boy enjoying this, watching humans suffer? He seemed to have no pity, no conscience at all.

The Prof answered from the canoe. He tried to make his voice sound casual, as if Ellis was just taking a walk in the park.

"Okay," he told Ellis. "See the ice in front of you. Tap it with the stick."

Ellis tapped at the ice. *Zing!* It made a loud musical note.

"That's the sound good ice makes," said the Prof. "You can walk ahead." As Ellis took a cautious few steps, the Prof shaded his eyes. It was hard to see properly. The sun made the ice flash like diamonds and he'd lost his sunglasses somewhere back on the river, in that wild water. He'd left the rope behind too – that was really sloppy. Ellis could have used it as a safety line.

Oh well, thought the Prof. *Never mind*.

He couldn't help it – he suddenly felt a dreamy indifference to his situation, as if nothing mattered, not even Ellis out on the ice...

Concentrate! The Prof shook himself, slapped his own face viciously. He had to fight the effects of hypothermia. He'd had to stay focused. Ellis's life depended on it.

"Stop!" he yelled to Ellis.

Out on the lake, Ellis didn't feel sleepy any more. He was wide awake, all his senses alert. He felt the ice rock under his feet, but knew he mustn't panic. He was already learning about ice. Just because it moved, didn't mean he'd fall through. He heard the Prof in the canoe behind him yell, "Tap again!"

Ellis tapped. This time the ice gave a dull *zonk.*

"That's bad ice! See the dark stain?" yelled the Prof as Ellis teetered on the edge of it. "Tap to your right instead."

Ellis tapped at a stretch of pearly blue ice: *zing!*

From the canoe the Prof yelled: "That's safe. Walk ahead!"

His nerves at screaming point, the Prof watched his ward's every step. He was concentrating so hard that he hardly noticed that his own body had stopped shaking.

"Walk ahead!" he yelled again. His voice was slurred. He could hardly move his blue lips. He tried to slap his own face again. But his hands were frozen into claws. His arms felt as heavy as bags of cement...

Ellis was walking ahead, getting closer to the tree-lined shore. His fear had gone now; his tracker's brain had taken over. *I'm getting the hang of this*, he thought. The ice was like any terrain he'd tracked before – desert, forest, mountains. If you looked for the signs, they told a story.

He tapped again, *zing!* – a high sweet note. It was as if the ice was talking to him, too, as if it had its own language. All you had to do was understand.

He knew he could walk safely ahead. But, automatically, he waited for the Prof's instructions. There weren't any.

Cautiously, he swivelled round on the ice. The Prof was sitting up in the canoe. But he wasn't watching Ellis – his head was drooping. And he was as still as an ice statue.

"Prof!" yelled Ellis. "Prof!"

There was no response.

He's fallen asleep, thought Ellis, his panic suddenly flooding back. What had the Prof said before? *If you fall asleep, you're as good as dead?*

Ellis didn't know what to do. Should he go back to the canoe, try to wake the Prof? Should he carry on to the shore, somehow force Blue to break his wintry spell?

He stared around, wildly, helplessly, a tiny figure all alone on a treacherous frozen lake.

"Meriel!" he screamed. "We're in trouble. You've got to help us!"

CHapTeR
THIRTeen

In the cave, Meriel heard Ellis shouting, "You've got to help us!"

That memory was still fresh in her mind – how the Prof had held onto her, even though she'd clawed his face, half blinded him.

No animal would have behaved like that, not if she'd hurt them as badly. They'd have run away and left her on dog island – or killed her right there, if they could.

Crazy humans, thought Meriel, snorting scornfully.

But, all the same, something was touched in her human heart. She snarled softly, as if trying to deny it. But she couldn't ignore Ellis's next near-hysterical call: "Meriel, the Prof's dying!"

She went racing out of the cave, on two legs now, not four. She didn't notice that Star and a few other greyhounds followed her.

Outside, she saw Blue on his rock. Her sharp eyes scanned the lake. She saw Ellis, near the shore, but stranded, it seemed, out on the ice. She saw the Prof sitting in the canoe, his head slumped.

Her human heart clenched with fear for them.

Then Ellis yelled out, "Blue's doing this! He's making the lake freeze up."

Meriel gazed astonished at Blue. Star had draped herself over his knees, he was hugging her neck. But at the same time, he was staring out over the lake, his eyes intense and focused, blazing with icy light.

"He hates humans," Ellis's shaky voice came again. "He's trying to kill us."

Meriel stared again at Blue. But she didn't have

to read his mind to feel his hatred. Or his power. It suddenly didn't amaze her at all that Blue could make winter come.

"Stop it, Blue!" she ordered.

Blue took his eyes off the lake for a second, turned round and growled at her. The other dogs growled too, as if to support him. Even Star bared her fangs at the child-puppy she'd given friendly licks to just moments ago in the cave.

And, in that moment, Meriel finally knew she'd been deceiving herself all along. She hadn't really found paradise here. With a stab of sorrow, she realized that she'd just been pretending, trying to recapture a life she'd lost long ago.

"Stop it, Blue!" she ordered him again. "They're my friends out there!"

Blue turned his back, as if she didn't exist. He fixed his luminous gaze on the lake again. Meriel's first impulse was to rush him, knock him off the rock. Maybe that would break his trance, end the spell.

But she knew, if she touched him, his dogs would turn on her. She didn't even trust Star not to attack. And if Blue barked for help, the whole pack would come pouring out of the cave to rip her to pieces.

So she forced herself to calm down and think. And suddenly she realized there was another way.

She closed her eyes and went into Blue's mind, searching for weaknesses, ways to make him stop.

After a few seconds, Meriel's eyes shot open. She'd found something deep in Blue's mind. Something that really surprised her. There'd been that fierce woman's face that suddenly turned to a mask of ice. Meriel had steeled herself for that. But there were other pictures, too, that she wasn't expecting – a warm cosy kitchen; a smiling old guy offering Blue food and drink.

Meriel made a wild guess: "Not all humans were cruel to you, were they, Blue? There was one who was kind."

At first, Meriel thought she was wrong, or that Blue didn't understand human speech. Because he didn't turn round, or show any response. But then Meriel saw his shoulders tighten. And he muttered one word: "Leon."

"Was that his name?" Meriel demanded, quick as a flash. "So would this Leon guy think killing people was okay? Would he say, 'Oh, just go ahead, Blue, well done'?"

Still Blue didn't turn round. Meriel was just thinking, *This is a waste of time,* that she'd have to rush him, despite the dogs, when suddenly Blue threw Star off his knees and bolted off the rock into the forest.

"Wait! Blue!" yelled Meriel. But she didn't go after him. She started racing round the shore, through the trees. As she ran, she saw the first drips coming off the icicles, felt the air warming up.

Blue's concentration, and his spell, was broken.

Out on the lake, Ellis was on the move again.

He had no idea what was going on between Blue and Meriel. He couldn't risk looking, he was concentrating too hard.

Zing! went the ice, as he tapped it with his stick. He stepped cautiously onto it.

He'd just made an agonizing choice. He was much closer to the shore than the canoe. He'd decided not to go back; that the best way to help the Prof was to get to Blue, as fast as he could.

"I'll stop that freak somehow!" vowed Ellis, through blue lips. He couldn't rely on Meriel. He wasn't even sure whose side she was on.

Zonk, went the ice. Not that way.

Only a few more metres to that pebble shore, with its snow-crusted pines.

"Don't hurry," Ellis warned himself. That way you made mistakes. And he wasn't safe yet. There was still deep water under this icy crust.

He made his numb fingers grip the stick. He tapped to test his next step. But this time the stick didn't clang off the ice with a *zing* or a *zonk.* Horrified, Ellis watched it pierce straight through and vanish in the dark water beneath.

At the same time, he felt the ice sagging beneath his shoes. Ellis swayed unsteadily. He daren't take another step.

With growing panic, he checked the shoreline. The ice looked different. It had been thick and milky before. Now it was turning transparent. Ellis could see water pulsing slowly through it, like blood through veins. He could see the lake underneath. Not black any more but green and clear.

It's thawing! thought Ellis. He risked a glance

along the lake. Blue wasn't there any more. He couldn't see Meriel either.

"Whoa!" cried Ellis, wobbling. Water was spurting up round his shoes. Any second now he'd plunge through, into water still cold enough to stop his heart.

Lie down, thought Ellis, frantically. *Spread your weight*.

Very carefully, he sank down on the ice, spreading out his weight like a starfish. He stayed perfectly still.

What now? he thought.

He began to slither towards the shore. He thought he was going to make it, he was almost there. But then the ice shifted sickeningly beneath him, sagging like a hammock. He was half submerged now, his legs sliding under.

"Grab hold," said a cool voice from the bank.

Ellis's hands scrabbled for the long branch pushed out towards him. He felt himself being pulled through slush. Then he was on a solid surface, sprawling on pebbles.

He rolled over, looked up into Meriel's face.

"The Prof!" he said.

He staggered up. Both of them stared across the lake to the canoe, where the Prof sat, hunched up, in the stern. Their keen eyes searched for any signs of movement. There weren't any.

"Think he's dead?" said Meriel, in her usual blunt way. Only her eyes betrayed the pain she felt.

"I'm swimming out there to see," said Ellis.

"No," said Meriel. She didn't want to lose Ellis, as well as the Prof. "The water's still too cold. Wait a few minutes."

All around them the big thaw continued at breakneck speed. The ice melted, the trees dripped, the wet ground steamed. The sun had heat again.

What was that noise filling her ears? Meriel tore her eyes away from the figure in the canoe. And realized that, across the lake, the waterfall was roaring again.

"I can't stand this," said Ellis. "I'm going out to him."

He waded into the water, where glittering coins of ice still floated.

"Wait," insisted Meriel.

Ellis gazed again at his guardian. "What? *What?*" he questioned Meriel frantically. "I can't see anything."

And then he saw it. The Prof's right hand was twitching. For a few nail-biting moments, nothing else happened. Then suddenly, like a jerky puppet, his head shot up.

"He's alive!" yelled Ellis joyfully.

He turned to face Meriel, a huge grin on his face. But she wasn't there. She was running back round the lake shore to search for Blue in the forest.

Ellis could see the Prof moving around, slapping his arms across his chest, trying to get his blood circulating.

"Ellis!" he yelled out, his voice very shaky.

"I'm here!" Ellis yelled from the shore. "I'm safe!"

The Prof saw something glittering in the water. It was his lost paddle, floating past. He reached out to get it. As he paddled slowly back, the mosquitoes were whining once more over the lake's surface. Summer had come back.

While he was busy setting his traps in the forest, Hunter had felt the chill. But Blue's powers had confined the freeze to a small area, as if the lake and the shore were in its own giant snow dome.

And Hunter was well away from the shore, deep among the trees.

It's just clouds covering the sun, Hunter thought, shivering.

But now the sun was out again, burning hot. Hunter wiped sweat off his brow as he finished setting his traps.

It was something he was very good at – he'd trapped animals all his life. His plan was to treat the wild kids just like any other prey and drive them into the forest, right into his snares. Or maybe he'd just snare one and grab the other. Every chase was different, you had to make split-second decisions. But, however it happened, Hunter was sure of one thing. That he'd catch those wild kids, no problem.

Chapter
Fourteen

Blue was running blindly through the forest.

After being hostile at first, he'd welcomed Meriel into his family. She spoke dog language – she seemed, like him, more animal than human. But now he just wanted to get away from her. With his dogs, life was black and white. He loved them, hated people – simple. But Meriel had messed up his mind, stirred up emotions deep inside him.

She'd reminded him about Leon, the one human he couldn't hate.

Blue stopped, quivering, his jaws dripping slaver. Was she following? He crouched, hiding among the forest ferns. He stayed there for some time, listening, his nose testing the air. He couldn't smell or hear her. He thought he was safe and stood up.

Then he heard a soft voice behind him say, "Blue."

He whipped round, snarling. She'd approached him silently and upwind, so he couldn't smell her.

Blue barked furiously, showed his fangs. His fierce, angry eyes flashed at her.

But Meriel stood her ground. She didn't flinch, or cower. Her angry eyes flashed back at him.

"Don't you start that freezing thing again," said Meriel severely.

Instantly, Blue dropped onto all fours. He whimpered at her, like a dog that's been beaten. His mind was in turmoil. He'd never met anyone like Meriel before. Her very presence seemed to weaken his powers.

Bewildered, he slunk off, under the trees. Meriel saw a sapling, suspiciously bent.

"No!" she shouted. "It's a trap!"

But Blue had put his head straight into the noose. A peg flipped out, the sapling swooshed upright. His eyes wide and terrified, Blue was jerked to his feet, the noose almost throttling him. He was on tiptoes now. His hands flew up, trying to pull it free.

Meriel was dashing to help him. But then Hunter stomped out of the trees and blocked her way. He couldn't believe his luck. Instead of having to stalk and chase his quarry it had come straight to him, just walked into one of his spring snare traps.

"I knew wild kids would be dumb," crowed Hunter, "but not as dumb as this."

When Blue saw Hunter he went crazy, trying to bite and claw him. But, with every movement, the noose tightened round his neck. Soon he was helpless, gasping and choking. Then Hunter moved in, and with two short lengths of cord, deftly tied Blue's wrists and ankles.

Blue writhed in his bonds, glaring hatred at Hunter. Like a dog pulling on a leash, it seemed he'd rather throttle himself than give in.

"Don't struggle, boy," Hunter told him. "Or you'll

strangle yourself. And I'm supposed to take you back alive."

Hunter turned his attention to Meriel.

She didn't run, so he thought he had her cowed. He strode confidently towards her. He stretched out a hand to grab her.

But Meriel skipped out of his reach. Then she threw back her head and howled.

Wolves use howls when they want sound to travel over long distances. And this was a particular kind of howl. It was urgent, high-pitched. Any dog would recognize it, from its wolf ancestry. It meant, *Come quickly! I need help*.

Hunter stopped and stared at her. Then he started laughing. He wiped the tears of mirth from his eyes. "Well, now I've seen everything! Where d'you learn to do that?"

Then he suddenly stopped laughing. His voice changed, became menacing. "Come here," he said to Meriel. "Bad dog."

Meriel glared at him defiantly. Hunter lost patience, lunged at her. Meriel skipped back again, just out of reach.

Behind Hunter, Blue had stopped struggling in

the trap. He'd suddenly become perfectly still.

Hunter and Meriel circled each other, like two fighters in a boxing ring. Hunter cursed, dived at Meriel. She dodged again. But, for a man mountain, he was horribly fast on his feet. She knew she couldn't keep taunting him for long.

She barked, so the greyhounds could home in on her voice.

Hunter lost his temper. "Stop doing that!" he said. "You're giving me the creeps."

Behind Hunter, Blue's eyes took on a luminous glow.

Hunter shivered. *Freaky weather*, shot through his mind. A white, spooky mist came drifting out of the trees.

Suddenly he decided he'd wasted enough time playing games. He reached for the hunting knife at his belt. Then he hesitated.

What's that? he thought. He could see dark shapes in the mist. *There! No, there!*

What's out there? he asked himself. He could feel his skin crawling. He drew his knife.

As he did, the first dog came sliding like a spectre out of the trees. It was the big white greyhound that had growled at Meriel in the cave.

Hunter recognized it too, as one of the dogs he'd been paid to poison.

"It – it can't be..." he stuttered to himself. The hand that held his knife was shaking. As far as he was concerned, that dog was dead.

Other dogs came bounding from the mist. As the pack gathered Hunter seemed frozen, his face white with shock.

Then Star trotted into the clearing, with her beautiful brindled coat, the dog he'd left for dead only two nights ago. She snarled at him, showing her sharp white fangs.

"Get them away from me!" cried Hunter, in a voice hoarse with horror. "Get them ghost dogs away from me!" Then he dropped his knife and fled, through the forest.

"Shouldn't have done that," murmured Meriel, as the pack streamed after him. "Stupid man, you can't outrun a greyhound."

She picked up the knife and ran over to Blue. She sliced through the rope that came down from the tree. Blue immediately collapsed into a gasping heap on the ground. After Meriel freed his wrists,

Blue tore the noose from round his own neck. He rubbed at the red welts on his throat, shook himself violently like a dog that's just been freed from its chain. Then he tore off the ties round his ankles and scuttled off, on all fours, after his dog family.

"Watch out for traps!" yelled Meriel. The mist was clearing, the temperature rising again as she raced after him.

She heard Hunter yelling, long before she saw him. He was dangling upside down from a birch tree, with a noose tight around both his feet. In his panicky rush to escape, he'd run straight into one of his own traps. And he didn't have his knife to free himself.

Around him, in a silent circle, stood Blue and the dogs, watching Hunter struggle. Even though he'd saved their lives, Blue didn't own the greyhounds, or control them. He was just part of the pack, playing, hunting, fighting like all the rest. But, this time, all the dogs seemed to defer to him. Even the big white dog seemed to look to Blue as leader. They could have rushed in and torn Hunter to pieces. But they didn't. They waited for Blue's decision.

As Meriel came sprinting into the clearing, Blue

gave it. He burst into a frenzy of short angry barks that meant, *Attack!*

The dogs crouched and snarled. Star was the first to hurl herself at Hunter.

On her first run she didn't bite him. She skidded to a stop right by his head, then made little rushes at him, barking like a mad dog, froth flying from her gaping jaws.

Hunter screamed and flapped his arms, twirling round on his rope each time Star came close.

Meriel stood watching, too. She knew that Star would make a couple more fake runs, then she'd bite Hunter for real. That would be the signal for all the other dogs to go rushing in. But then she heard a voice in her ear. It was cool but authoritative. It said, "Meriel, tell Blue to call the dogs off."

"Hello, Prof," said Meriel. She gave a nod to Ellis who was beside him.

The Prof's face was deathly pale, and he was shaking badly. But he was pleased about that. It showed he was back in the land of the living. He knew he was lucky to have survived those sub-zero temperatures.

"Meriel, did you hear what I said?"

Meriel sighed. "Yes, Prof."

She would have liked to see the dogs getting their revenge. But she knew the Prof wouldn't stand for that. Meriel didn't know the right dog language, so she used human speech. "Call off the dogs," she told Blue.

Blue understood. But he didn't obey. Why shouldn't the dogs kill Hunter? He was their enemy. He'd kill them if he got the chance. He'd tried to once already.

"Meriel!" the Prof insisted. Star had rushed in again, stopped. Now she was sniffing the back of Hunter's neck. Hunter's yells got louder as he felt her hot, doggy breath.

Suddenly Star backed off again, stopped her manic barking. She crouched down silently, fangs bared. Her next run wouldn't be fake.

Meriel had moved closer to Blue. She whispered one word in Blue's ear: "Leon." Blue stared at her with stricken eyes, as if she'd betrayed him, bringing up his human past again to complicate things.

But as Star sprang, Blue barked. Star twisted in mid-air and dropped to the ground. She gazed at

Blue accusingly. Her eyes said, *Why did you call me off?*

Star and the other dogs twitched restlessly, as the Prof took the knife from Meriel and cut Hunter down. The dogs were excited, their eyes bright, their pink tongues hanging out, panting. But they didn't attack.

"If I were you," the Prof said to Hunter, "I'd say nothing about this back at Forest Edge. Just say you searched, but there was no wild boy in the forest. Do you understand?"

Hunter nodded dumbly.

"You don't do as he says," added Ellis, "the ghost dogs will come and get you. Wherever you are. Wherever you hide, they'll find you."

Hunter staggered to his feet, gave one appalled glance at the dogs and ran off, crashing through the trees.

"Huh!" said Meriel, disgusted. "He got off far too easy!"

"I don't think so," the Prof disagreed. "He'll suffer. He'll never sleep easy in his bed again. And he's lost all credibility as the town's tough guy. He's just a laughing stock."

The dogs were itching to chase Hunter again. But Blue gave one sharp bark and they came slinking back.

What happens now? Ellis was thinking.

He'd wanted to take Blue home to live with them. But now he knew it would never work. Blue wasn't only a feral child. He was something much more awesome and sinister. He had the power to control nature.

Even now, Blue was turning those weird, ice-blue eyes towards them and Ellis could feel the air temperature falling.

The Prof tugged Ellis's arm and whispered, "Let's leave Blue and Meriel alone for a minute."

"What if he tries to freeze her?" hissed Ellis.

"I don't think he'll do that," said the Prof.

Ellis and the Prof backed off into the trees, leaving Blue and Meriel, both standing upright, staring at each other. The greyhounds twined around them, sniffing at them, licking their hands. Now the other humans had gone, the hatred went from Blue's eyes.

He couldn't figure Meriel out. Was she more dog, or more human? She sent out such mixed messages.

But she'd freed him from Hunter's trap. That was something he'd never forget.

He suddenly barked at Meriel, a joyous bark of invitation that meant, *Come with us.*

"I can't," said Meriel.

Blue stared at her.

"I just can't," said Meriel, sharply. She didn't know the dog language to explain the struggle going on inside her. Or the human language either.

Blue shrugged, as if to say, *Your loss*, and, without speaking to her again, slid off into the trees. The greyhounds loped after him.

Meriel stood gazing after them, knowing her chance was gone. Her head told her she'd made the right choice, that she could never recapture the past. But that didn't help the pain in her heart.

After a few minutes, the Prof and Ellis came to join her.

"Blue's gone," said Meriel.

"Gone?" said Ellis. "Didn't you try to stop him?"

"No," said Meriel. "Couldn't even if I'd wanted to. And I didn't want to," she added, defiantly.

She didn't say any more. But the Prof heaved a long, deep sigh of relief. He'd deliberately left Meriel alone so she could make her own decisions. So she could leave with Blue if she wanted to. But he was filled with secret happiness that she hadn't.

"But where is Blue heading?" asked Ellis.

"To the north?" suggested the Prof. "Further away from people?"

There were bigger forests further north and they were much more remote, not near any towns.

"I could track them," said Ellis. "Find out for certain."

"No," Meriel insisted, with that stubborn glint in her eyes. "Leave them alone."

"I just hope he stays away from people," murmured the Prof, frowning. Blue could be a danger to people. The Prof knew he should probably alert the police. But he couldn't bear to think of Blue locked away for the rest of his life. Or experimented on in a laboratory because of his amazing powers.

"He will stay away from people," said Meriel. "Blue doesn't need people. He's got his dogs."

The Prof still looked unsure. If Blue and his dogs could find a peaceful place – where they could live undisturbed by people – then they might stand a chance. But were there any places like that left in the world?

If anything happens, the Prof thought privately, *if there are any reports of freak snowstorms in high summer, then I'll have to tell the police.*

But now wasn't the time to share his fears about Blue's future. Instead the Prof told his wards, "Let's go home. This mission is over, as far as we're concerned."

The three of them went back to the lake shore, where the Prof had left the canoe.

"We'll paddle on downriver to the next town," said the Prof. "Get a taxi back to Forest Edge, pick up my car."

"Can we grab something to eat there?" said Ellis. "I'm starving."

As they canoed off the lake, Meriel swivelled round in her seat. She took one last glance at the sparkling waterfall and the abandoned cave behind it.

From somewhere deep in the forest came a distant howl.

It's Blue, thought Meriel, a quiver running through her.

She sniffed the air, threw back her head like a wolf. But she didn't call back.

CHAPTER
FIFTEEN

Late one night, the phone rang in the Prof's flat at the Natural History Museum.

"It's JJ," said the Prof. He held out the phone to Ellis. "He wants to talk to you."

Ellis frowned. "What for?"

It was two weeks since they'd come back from Forest Edge. Ellis was busy planning another mission. He'd almost forgotten about JJ – the boy reporter who'd do anything to get a scoop.

"Hello, JJ," said Ellis, warily. "Is Hunter in jail yet? Did the Forest Edge Echo bring him to justice?"

"What, for dog poisoning?" said JJ. "We didn't have enough evidence. You never found me a dog's body, did you? Anyway, Hunter's not here any more. His shack's empty. He moved out – who cares where he went?"

"So what do you want, JJ?" asked Ellis.

"I thought long and hard about calling you," declared JJ. "Specially after you messed things up, getting yourself caught by Hunter. I mean how stupid was that? And being wrong about the wild boy."

"What do you mean wrong?" said Ellis.

"Hunter said he doesn't exist. Else he'd have found him for sure. Anyhow, I'm not interested in wild boys now. Something better has come up."

"Another scoop?" said Ellis.

"Yeah! A real one this time. And I need a tracker. So I've decided to give you another chance."

"Gee thanks, JJ," said Ellis.

"I can see the headlines now," said JJ, rushing on, excitedly. *"The Wild Beast of Forest Edge*! We've got photos. It looks huge and fierce, maybe an escaped panther! Or a man-eating lion! Dad's going to love it!"

"JJ," interrupted Ellis, "I've heard those wild beast stories before. They're a waste of time. It always turns out to be somebody's big fat pussycat."

"You mean you won't track it for me?" said JJ. His voice sounded disbelieving. He was Jay Harding Junior. Nobody turned him down!

"No, JJ," said Ellis. "Get some other mug."

Ellis put down the phone. He turned to the Prof. "The pressure's off Blue," he said. "No one's looking for him now. Hunter told everyone there was no wild boy."

"Good," said the Prof.

"Is there any news about Blue?" asked Ellis.

"No, nothing," said the Prof. There'd been no news from the north. No one had spotted a wild boy with a dog pack. Or reported any freak weather conditions. Blue seemed to have vanished from the face of the earth.

There was silence for a moment between them. Then Ellis asked the Prof, "How did Blue do it? Make winter come like that, whenever he wanted?"

This very question had been tormenting the Prof. He couldn't stop thinking about it, researching possible explanations. But he was still no closer to an answer than Ellis.

"Of course we've got no actual evidence it was him," the Prof began, cautiously.

"Come on!" Ellis butted in. "Course we have! Meriel went into his mind. She was sure it was him."

"I know," said the Prof. "But I was looking for more *scientific* proof," he admitted. "Anyway, talking about Meriel, where is she? I haven't seen her for a while. Has she gone walkabout again?"

"I don't know," said Ellis. "But there's something she told me. She knows that she blinded you, made you lose your eye. She remembered about it, in the cave, with the dogs."

"Oh no," sighed the Prof. "I was afraid of that. So what did you say?"

"I said, 'Look, Meriel, don't lose sleep about it. Don't feel guilty.'"

"So what did *she* say?" asked the Prof, looking anxious. All these years, it had haunted him that if Meriel found out the truth, she'd never forgive herself.

"Well," replied Ellis. "She sort of stared at me, like I was speaking a strange language. Then she said, 'Guilty? I don't understand.'"

The Prof looked perplexed for a second, then burst out laughing. "That's my Meriel," he said.

Why had he worried all this time about her reaction? He should have known that, like animals, Meriel didn't do guilt. Nothing spoiled *her* sleep. Except mind-reading nocturnal predators, of course.

Five floors above their heads, Meriel crouched on the flat roof of the Natural History Museum. Like many wild creatures, Meriel felt safe high up, where she could keep a good lookout.

Above her was a navy blue night sky. Spread all around her was the city, a maze of blurred and twinkling lights. From up here, the roar of its traffic was just a murmur. But Meriel was looking straight down, into the garden of the Natural History Museum.

She heard a series of short, savage shrieks. Meriel shivered with excitement.

"An owl hunting," she told herself happily.

She leaned out dangerously far, over the roof edge. Her eyes scanned the dark treetops. She saw fierce golden eyes flash among the branches.

"There you are, owl," she grinned. "I've found you."

And, suddenly, she was whisked clean out of her own head.

Something slid up inside her throat. "*Hakk!*" She gave a tiny cough, then spewed it out. It was a neat little pellet of the bones of her last meal, a frog. Now she was hungry again. Time to go hunting.

She heard rustling. Her head swivelled, almost in a circle. There! Her great saucer eyes locked on. Now she was gliding down, a swift, silent killer.

She felt wind in her feathers, her talons stretched out. She swooped, dropped like a stone. The rat struggled frantically, but a snap of her beak stopped that.

"Awww," sighed Meriel, as she watched the owl gliding back over the trees, with the dead rat dangling from its claws. She was back in her own mind, as suddenly as she'd left. Why couldn't she control this mind-reading thing better? She'd wanted to fly some more, to feel herself soaring on air currents, cradled by the warm night winds. Flying was one of her favourite things.

But the owl had gone now. Meriel lifted her eyes and stared out northwards, over the city, to the dark countryside beyond.

Where are you, Blue? she wondered.

She couldn't mind-read him, of course. He and the dogs were impossibly far away, maybe hundreds of kilometres by now.

She threw back her head and howled like a wolf at the moon. She knew Blue couldn't hear her but it made her feel better.

She felt no self-pity. Meriel never did. But deep in her heart she *did* sense something.

She sensed she hadn't seen the last of Blue.

She was sure that sometime, somewhere, maybe on another mission, she and the wild boy would meet again.

Don't miss
more incredible missions
with the
ANIMAL INVESTIGATORS...

ANIMAL INVESTIGATORS:
MISSION 1

RED EYE

Mission:

To find out the truth about the evil RED EYE.

File notes:

A half-crazed boy has turned up at HQ, raving about an army of gulls taking over his town, led by the malevolent Red Eye.

Ellis and Meriel must determine whether the story is true. Then utilize their special powers and animal expertise to stop the deadly menace from terrorizing the town's people.

Out now!

ISBN 9780746085752

£5.99

ANIMAL INVESTIGATORS:
MISSION 3

KILLER SPIDERS

Mission:

To stop the terrifying KILLER SPIDERS.

File notes:

An old friend of the Prof has barricaded himself inside his own bio-dome. On a live TV link he says everything's fine, but his desperate messages to his son say something different. Has his experiment been invaded by nightmare creatures?

Ellis and Meriel must find a way into the dome and face the fearsome threat that it contains.

Coming soon...
ISBN 9780746096130
£5.99

For more thrilling
mystery adventures
log on to
www.fiction.usborne.com